Anonymous

Memorial addresses on the life and character of Henry Bowen Anthony

A senator from Rhode Island - Volume I

Anonymous

Memorial addresses on the life and character of Henry Bowen Anthony
A senator from Rhode Island - Volume I

ISBN/EAN: 9783744731560

Printed in Europe, USA, Canada, Australia, Japan

Cover: Foto ©Raphael Reischuk / pixelio.de

More available books at **www.hansebooks.com**

MEMORIAL ADDRESSES

LIFE AND CHARACTER

OF

HENRY BOWEN ANTHONY

(A SENATOR FROM RHODE ISLAND),

DELIVERED IN THE

SENATE AND HOUSE OF REPRESENTATIVES,

FORTY-EIGHTH CONGRESS, SECOND SESSION,

JANUARY 19 AND 21, 1885,

WITH

THE FUNERAL SERVICES AT PROVIDENCE, RHODE ISLAND,
SEPTEMBER 6, 1884.

———◆———

WASHINGTON:
GOVERNMENT PRINTING OFFICE.
1885.

AN ACT to authorize the printing of the eulogies delivered in Congress upon the late Henry B. Anthony.

Be it enacted by the Senate and House of Representatives of the United States of America in Congress assembled, That there be printed of the eulogies delivered in Congress upon the late Henry B. Anthony, a Senator from Rhode Island, with an account of his funeral, prepared under the direction of the Joint Committee on Public Printing, twelve thousand copies, of which four thousand shall be for the use of the Senate and eight thousand for the use of the House of Representatives; and the Secretary of the Treasury is hereby directed to have printed a portrait of said Henry B. Anthony to accompany said eulogies; and for engraving and printing said portrait the sum of five hundred dollars, or so much as may be necessary, is hereby appropriated out of any money in the Treasury not otherwise appropriated.

Approved, March 3, 1885.

2

THE FUNERAL SERVICES,

At Providence, Rhode Island, September 6, 1884.

Henry Bowen Anthony, the senior Senator from Rhode
Island, died at his home in the city of Providence September
2, 1884. Appropriate action was taken by the State and municipal authorities, the Board of Trade, the Press Club, and
other local associations, and the arrangements for the funeral
were directed by Colonel W. P. Canaday, Sergeant-at-Arms
of the United States Senate.

The funeral took place on Saturday, September 6. The
national flag hung at half-mast from the flag-staffs of the public
buildings and of many private residences, and the windows of
the principal stores were draped in mourning. The city hall,
the custom-house, the post-office, the United States, State, and
municipal courts, and several large manufactories, with nearly
all of the large business houses, were closed at noon, and a
Sunday quiet prevailed in the central part of the city.

THE FUNERAL SERVICES.

The funeral services were held in the First Congregational
church, on Benefit street. The doors were opened at eleven
o'clock, and the seats not reserved were soon filled. Among
those who soon took the seats assigned to them were His Ex-
cellency Governor Bourn, attended by his staff; ex-governors of

3

Rhode Island; Baron de Struve, the Russian Minister; United States and State judges, the municipal authorities of Providence, the faculty of Brown University, the directors of the American National Bank, committees of the Mechanics' Exchange, the Providence Press Club, and the employés of the Providence Journal.

At noon the casket containing the remains of the deceased Senator was brought from his late neighboring residence into the church by six stalwart policemen. They were attended by the honorary pall-bearers: Colonel William Goddard, Professor William Gammell, Judge Walter S. Burges, Colonel G. H. Browne, ex-Governor C. C. Van Zandt, ex-Governor W. W. Hoppin, Postmaster Henry W. Gardner, and Edward H. Hazard, esq. A committee of the United States Senate, which followed the casket, preceded by Colonel W. P. Canaday, their Sergeant-at-Arms, was composed of the Honorables Nelson W. Aldrich, Justin S. Morrill, George F. Hoar, Henry L. Dawes, Austin F. Pike, Joseph R. Hawley, John R. McPherson, J. Donald Cameron, Isham G. Harris, Charles W. Jones, James L. Pugh, M. C. Butler, Thomas F. Bayard, and Matt W. Ransom. With them were General Anson G. McCook, Secretary of the Senate; Isaac Bassett, assistant doorkeeper; James I. Christie, deputy sergeant-at-arms; Thomas W. Manchester, messenger; Henry A. Pierce, assistant financial clerk; and Ben: Perley Poore, clerk of printing records. Then came the relatives and personal friends of the deceased, the special committee of the general assembly of Rhode Island, the household servants of the deceased, and prominent citizens of Rhode Island.

The remains were met at the door of the church by its pastor, the Rev. Thomas R. Slicer, accompanied by the Rev.

Augustus Woodbury, pastor of the Westminster church, Providence, and the Rev. E. D. Huntley, Chaplain of the United States Senate, who preceded the casket down the middle aisle, reciting the burial service, while the organist performed "The Dead March in Saul." The massive pulpit-front was draped with crape, while on the communion table rested a floral cross on which was the symbolic anchor of Rhode Island. A sheaf of ripened wheat rose from a base of varied flowers, and there was a pillow of white roses, while resting on the casket was a wreath of rare exotics.

After the casket had been deposited in front of the pulpit, and the pall-bearers had taken their seats, Chester A. Arthur, President of the United States, came in by a side door, accompanied by the Hon. George F. Edmunds, President *pro tempore* of the United States Senate; the Hon. Benjamin Harris Brewster, Attorney-General of the United States, and the Hon. David Davis, of Illinois.

The services were begun with an original anthem, "Whatever My God Ordains is Right," composed for the occasion by Mr. Eben Kelley and sung by the quartet choir. What is known as the "Boston King's Chapel Service" was used. The Rev. Mr. Slicer read appropriate selections from the Scriptures, after which the choir sang Senator ANTHONY's favorite hymn, "Lead, kindly light." The Rev. Dr. Huntley followed with a fervent prayer, after which the congregational hymn, "Thou, Grace Divine, encircling all," was sung.

ADDRESS BY THE REV. AUGUSTUS WOODBURY.

The Rev. Mr. WOODBURY said:

The silent and secret forces of insidious disease are among those mysterious elements of our physical being which seem to baffle human skill. The physician faithfully studies the problem, but can only approximate its solution. Death, by slow degrees, saps the foundation, and in due time overthrows the structure of life. Nature gradually succumbs; the inevitable hour approaches with sure steps; the organs of the body cease to discharge their functions; the eyes look their last upon the faces of dear friends; the spirit exhales, and there is nothing left but the rigid form, soon to change to dust and ashes. When death comes suddenly we who remain are stunned by the shock, and cannot make real to our hearts and minds the departure of our friend from the scenes in which he was a familiar object of our affection and regard. But in the progress of long-continued sickness we sadly watch and wait, in the anxiety of a protracted suspense, the fond eye of love catching the glimpse of every favorable symptom, hoping against hope, or noting, with quick and sympathetic recognition, the gradual failure of the physical powers, till the fatal change comes and leaves the heart bereaved.

All this we say is the Providential ordering, and we submit to the decrees of that Almighty Power which joins with its action the designs of infinite wisdom and the exercise of infinite love. To the sufferer himself who is obliged to feel that death cannot be averted, although its coming may be somewhat delayed, the experience is not without its compensations. Human intelligence cannot devise a remedy, but Divine Providence furnishes an alleviation in the training of character. Patience, courage, trust, obedience, are cultivated in the soul. "Not as I will" becomes the habitual expression of the heart—difficult to say with a full comprehension of its meaning, but when completely realized, the sublime word of a victorious faith. To be weak is to be miserable! It is quite true, for ambition is quenched, energy is dissipated, mental and physical activity is stopped, and one is forced to be a spectator merely of scenes in which he would gladly have taken part, and to confess that his work in the world is done. Yet this weakness may be re-enforced by the divine presence and power, and the spirit may be lifted up into a plane of life from which it can look serenely down upon the weaknesses and pains of this mortal state, and prepare itself for the entrance into immortal life. For death, as we are assured, is not the end. It is the transition stage of the soul, the door which opens to the spirit the boundless realm of immortality.

Do I err in saying that to our friend, whose obsequies we observe to-day, this discipline of the spirit has been exercised for his eternal good? The disease to which he has yielded was certain in its progress, and its end was calmly foreseen. He could not have deceived himself by any flattering indications of temporary improvement. He has himself anticipated the hour when his physical life would be extinguished. Perhaps he may have preferred to die at the capital; possibly in the Senate Chamber itself, the scene of his patriotic labors, in the midst of associates who had learned both to honor and to love him. For men, who, when living, serve the state with passionate devotion, may fittingly desire to die on the spot which has been rendered memorable by their presence—as the soldier would wish to fall upon the field of battle, or the man of God would wish to be stricken down wearing the harness of his valiant endeavor for the divine kingdom. But, whenever and wherever the summons might come, he was ready. With a cheerful courage, with a patient submission, with an undoubting trust, he has calmly looked forward to the time of his departure from the field of active life. For him death had no terrors, for he had schooled himself to that serenity of soul which could not be disturbed either in life or death. Not given much to introspection, certainly not disposed to make public his private and personal experiences, he was yet, without doubt, conscious in himself of this calm and peaceful state, and thus passed painlessly and quietly to his final rest. Long has he filled the public eye, well has he accomplished the mission of his public service, faithfully has he discharged the public trusts committed to his care, and now he leaves to his fellow-citizens and his fellow-countrymen the record of his diligent and devoted labor. We attempt no labored panegyric. We pass no judgment. The future will determine the value of his service, and posterity will pronounce the verdict, "Well done!" To speak a simple word of appreciation, before the grave shall shut him from our sight, is the office of the hour.

Mr. ANTHONY was a genuine child and a faithful representative of Rhode Island. Born upon her soil, nurtured in her traditions, educated at her university, receiving the highest honors she had to give, he thoroughly believed in the perfection of her policy and the permanence of her institutions. When called upon to defend the peculiar features of her government, he brought to the task both the ability of an advocate and the devotion of a son. In the editorial chair of the journal which he controlled, and in his seat in the Senate, he never forgot the obligations he owed to the mother who had reared and raised him to the position which he occupied and filled. He was jealous of her honor and was always prepared to do valiant battle for her ancient prerogatives. The arguments which more than once he made both in the Journal and in the Senate in her behalf may not have wholly convinced those who believed that in the changes of the times a more generous extension of suffrage and a freer commercial policy were desirable. But no one could question the depth of his convictions and the sincerity of his faith. He was positive that the prosperity of the State and the welfare of its people were bound up in the maintenance of institutions which its history had sanctioned. With the power of this assurance, he went to his duty with an unflinching resolution to give to it the fullest ability he could command. This element of strength is not to be lightly valued in making up the estimate of his character.

But the claims of his native State were not permitted to lessen his devotion to his country's need. His patriotism was as wise and enlightened as it was eminent and marked. Entering the Senate at a time when the first mutterings of the storm that was to sweep the land were heard, he was prepared with a calm courage to face the tempest when it broke. Feeling the full sense of the responsibility of the occasion, as a representative of the Union, he was fearless and urgent in all measures for the defense of free institutions and the preservation of the Republic. He never doubted the result of the struggle in its darkest days, but cheerfully and bravely wrought on for the achievement of a full success. In the days of reconstruction he endeavored so to work that no misfortunes of a similar kind might befall. The constitution of the Senate changed. One by one his early associates passed away. Some paid the debt of Nature. Others were swept away by political revolutions. But no revolutions touched his seat or alienated the support of the people of his State. Repeated re-elections returned him to his Senatorial chair. He became the " Father of the Senate," and as the new members came in they sought both his counsel and his friendship. He was elected President *pro tempore*, and with grace and dignity he conducted the deliberations of the distinguished body which called him to its chief post of honor. It was something more than a compliment when the Senate, notwithstanding his precarious health, delayed its organization, and once more elected him to the office, hoping that he might be able to discharge its duties. It was a recognition of his worth, and though he was obliged to decline the position, he was touched with gratitude and made more conscious than ever of the warmth of feeling which his fellow-members cherished towards him in their hearts. He was the model legislator of the upper branch of the National Congress, not indulging in long debate, but always attentive and always present in the spirit of conscious duty. His practical wisdom is perpetuated in the rule for facilitating the business of the Senate which bears his name.

Public life has many temptations, and there have been men in public station who have thought it not beneath them to serve themselves and their own interest while engaged in serving the state. It is true that many stories that are bandied about in the public press, with too ready an appetite for scandal, are gross exaggerations. In the fierce light that beats upon official station peccadilloes become crimes. Of these, indeed, we condone nothing, we excuse nothing. But partisan zeal may sometimes put a wrong construction upon innocent motives and acts. Happily for ourselves, we have no need to speak here with bated breath. For honor has followed merit and the laurel bears no blighted leaf. Of the value and honesty of Mr. ANTHONY'S public service there has never been the slightest question. No breath of detraction ever tarnished the luster of his well-earned public fame. He did not seek or use his office for private gain or personal emolument. If he did not rise—or even aspire to rise—to the summit of the highest statesmanship, he yet allowed no one to surpass him in the singleness of his purpose to advance the interests of his State and to promote the welfare of his country. His stainless patriotism and his unsullied public service are known of all men. They are as creditable to the people of our Commonwealth as to himself. The representative reflects the character of his constituents. If the fountain of public virtue be pure, the stream cannot well be turbid.

It seems but commonplace to speak of Mr. ANTHONY's literary attainments. Accepting journalism as his profession, he rapidly carried the paper which he edited to the foremost rank. Soon after he took charge of it, there came on a period of great public disturbance, when the safety of the Commonwealth really trembled in the balance. He gave such direction to public sentiment and such encouragement to the cause of public order as to merit the generous recognition of his labors which his fellow-citizens were glad to give. With a clear, incisive, direct style of composition, he brought to the daily discussion of current events and public measures the ample stores and full equipment of a well-furnished mind. He brightened the columns of the Journal with delicate humor and lambent wit. When indulging in satire, he carried in the velvet scabbard of his well-turned periods a sword sharp as the scimiter of Saladin. In the consideration of graver themes he exhibited a cogency and vigor which revealed the strength of an original and carefully-trained intellect. If one should meet him in controversy, it were well to see that there were no weak or unguarded places in the joints of the armor. For his keen eye was sure to find them and his trenchant blade would be thrust home with fatal result. His election as governor did not take him from his daily labor, while he neglected no public duty. During the intervals of relief from his official labors at Washington, even when aided by the graceful and accomplished scholar who now presides over the University of Michigan, he was still active in editorial work. It was not till the advent of his late associate, whose recent death was like the loss of his right arm, that he may be said to have relinquished the management of the Journal. Its columns were enriched by frequent contributions from his ready pen. After Mr. Danielson resumed control, the daily mail brought to the office the letter which he found time amidst engrossing cares to write. He loved the Journal, for it was his offspring.

His fellow-Senators will in due time bear witness to the excellence and variety of these literary gifts. In a larger field, on a more conspicuous stage, the same qualities of mind and heart were displayed. He did not often speak at length. It would be far from his habit to occupy an entire session with prolonged address. But when he spoke it was from a thorough knowledge of his subject, and in pregnant and weighty words. His long experience and his accurate acquaintance with public affairs gave him a commanding influence. He was well entitled to the respect and attention with which he was always heard. His work in the committee-room was thorough and efficient, and the public measures which he brought to the Senate, well digested and prepared, were accepted as the conclusions of one who knew well the true character and purpose of national legislation.

In one department of public speaking he certainly excelled. The memorial addresses which from time to time he delivered in the Senate are among the finest specimens of elegiac oratory to be found in our language. In this he discharged no perfunctory duty. Speaking from the heart, with a delicate appreciation of character, with a marvelous felicity of diction and facility of expression, with a complete and clear conception of the gravity of the occasion, he uttered the sincere sentiments of brotherly affection and friendly regard. Of these the three addresses which he made on the death of Senator Sumner are pre-eminent. It became his duty to deliver to the authorities of Massachusetts the body of the deceased statesman. I have been told by the Sergeant-at-Arms of the Senate, who accompanied the committee to Boston, that Mr. ANTHONY was not informed till reaching the frontier of the State of what was expected of him. Amidst the noise and turmoil of the railway journey he composed in his mind the brief but touching address which deserves to be inscribed on the imperishable bronze. It was the grateful expression of profound feeling when, in committing to the governor of our neighboring Commonwealth the mortal part of her honored son, he further said:

The part which we do not return to you is not wholly yours to receive, nor altogether ours to give. It belongs to the country, to freedom, to civilization, to humanity.

The heart of the man spoke from the tongue, and when on other occasions he addressed the Senate in eulogy of the friends who had fallen by his side, we may well believe that his whole being was stirred by the warm emotions that found expression on his eloquent lips.

Glimpses of his inner life are thus vouchsafed to us. And if we were permitted here to enter into those sacred precincts, where personal and private sorrow has its home, there would be a full revelation of kindness, gentle consideration, fraternal love, generous helpfulness, loyal friendship, and uplifting faith. An early sorrow touched our friend soon after he had entered upon his public career. There is no doubt but that it tinged

all his subsequent years.   For though in social intercourse he
was a most genial host, an ever-welcome guest, a delightful
companion, and the center of a charmed and charming circle of
friends, there was still the unseen presence of a melancholy
which checked the exuberance of his spirits.   It was the minor
chord in the harmony of his life.   It is not for me to dwell
upon the theme.   Those who have through life felt the warm
contact of his love, who have experienced the joy of his
friendship, who have shared his confidence and secured his
esteem, carry in their hearts the fervent, grateful appreciation of his virtue, and will long cherish the memory of his
worth.   Those who were associated with him in the common
duties and labors of humanity, those who were employed by
him in the conduct of his chosen occupation, those who for
many years have looked. upon him as a master and leader in
their business, will acknowledge the justice and honor with
which every detail was observed, the fidelity with which every
obligation was met, and the thoroughness with which every
task was performed.   Three-score years and ten have nearly
passed.   The heavy burden has been laid down.   The weary
body is at rest.   The busy mind has transferred its activity to
another sphere of being.   The spirit is with its God.

Mr. ANTHONY has seen in the Senate a generation of states-
men pass away.   He has seen a new generation come upon the
stage of public life.   Is the past better than the present?   As
we bid farewell to those who vanish from our sight, have we
no word of welcome to those who are pressing forward?   We
grieve over the death of men who we hardly thought could be
spared.   We look around to see who are to take up and carry
on the work which they have been doing.   A pillar of the
state has fallen, and as we look upon the fragments we fear

that the structure is weakened. But the Republic, bereaved afresh of one of its most trusted and trustworthy counselors, still lives. Divine Providence finds its agents and instruments, and by the inspiration and help of the Divine presence the blessed results for humanity will be attained. I cannot more fittingly close this address than in Mr. ANTHONY'S own words:

When I recall those whom I have seen fall around me, and whom I thought necessary to the success, almost to the preservation of great principles, I recall also those whom I have seen step into the vacant places, put on the armor which they wore, lift the weapons which they wielded, and march on to the consummation of the work which they inaugurated. And thus I am filled with reverent wonder at the beneficent ordering of nature and inspired with a loftier faith in that Almighty Power without whose guidance and direction all human effort is vain, and with whose blessing the humblest instruments that He selects are equal to the mightiest work that He designs.

After the address a congregational hymn was sung, and the benediction was pronounced by the Rev. Mr. Slicer. The remains were then taken to the Swan Point Cemetery, followed by a long procession of carriages, and were there entombed.

PROCEEDINGS IN THE SENATE.

MONDAY, JANUARY 19, 1885.

THE PRAYER.

The Chaplain, Rev. E. D. Huntley, D. D., offered the following prayer:

Let us pray. Almighty God, our Heavenly Father, we come again to worship before Thee; and we pray that Thou wilt so dispose our minds that the words of our mouth and the meditation of our hearts may be acceptable in Thy sight. Our iniquities have separated between us and our God; and that we are at all tolerated as worshipers in Thy presence is another proof of that long suffering which ages ago was proclaimed as one of the distinguishing characteristics of Thy nature.

Thou art He by whom kings reign and princes decree justice. Thou art pleased to carry out Thy purposes in no small part by the governments which men, under the direction of God-implanted impulses, have established throughout the earth. One of these governments is represented in this Chamber, and we pray that the legislation of this body may be so under Thy control that the history of the nation, so far as may be learned by the proceedings here, may show us striving to become a people whose God shall be the Lord.

We are this day to be reminded of the uncertainties of life. Members of the Senate shall rise in their places to honor the

memory of the distinguished dead. They shall recount his
virtues; they shall emphasize the intellectual and moral characteristics which eminently fitted him for the high position he
occupied so long and with such credit to himself and to the
country; and we humbly pray that this recital may stir us
up to such a consecration of our talents as shall develop an
absolutely faithful service to the nation for the days that are
to come.

And do Thou help us so to spend the few days which remain
to us upon the earth that the discriminating eulogist may pronounce upon our personal and political career, as he in candor
must this day pronounce upon the career of him we mourn, the
benedictions of a grateful and appreciative country.

And, more than this, may the services we shall be able
humbly to render to the nation be impelled by such a desire
to please the nation's God that, while men shall speak well
of what has been, it shall please Thee to pronounce blessings
upon us during the ages yet to be. We ask it in the name of
Him who is the resurrection and the life. Amen.

Mr. ALDRICH, of Rhode Island. In accordance with previous
notice, I offer the following resolutions and ask for their present consideration:

Resolved, That the Senate has heard with profound sorrow of the death of HENRY
B. ANTHONY, late a Senator from the State of Rhode Island.

Resolved, That the business of the Senate be now suspended, to enable his associates to pay proper tribute of regard to his high character and distinguished public
services.

Resolved, That the Secretary of the Senate communicate these resolutions to the
House of Representatives.

Resolved, That, as an additional mark of respect to the memory of the deceased, the
Senate do now adjourn.

Remarks by Mr. ALDRICH, of Rhode Island.

Mr. PRESIDENT: He who was here the senior in service, and first in the affections of his associates rests in

The lone couch of his everlasting sleep.

His great heart with all its attractive qualities has ceased to beat. His stalwart form, so recently instinct with strength and life, is crumbling in the dust.

He who has so often lighted up with the touches of matchless eloquence the character of others is no more. Suffering from a sense of personal loss which is beyond expression, and from the sorrow of separation from a wise councilor and faithful friend, I despair of rendering an adequate tribute of praise to his memory.

HENRY BOWEN ANTHONY was born at Coventry, Rhode Island, April 1, 1815. His ancestors had for more than a century and a half resided on Rhode Island soil. His father, William Anthony, and his maternal grandfather, James Greene, were Quakers. His father was a cotton manufacturer, and the establishment of which he was the manager was the third of its kind erected in the State.

William Anthony was a man of strong character, greatly respected by his neighbors, and it is easy to trace the influence of his wise teachings and watchful care in the future character of the son. The latter was, in his early life, imbued with the doctrines of the Society of Friends, which left their impress on his nature, developing that gentleness of manner and love of peaceful methods, that strict integrity and conscientious devotion to duty, which were the most striking traits of his character.

He received a preparatory education at a private school in Providence, and entered Brown University in 1829. At college he had the benefit of the teachings of the distinguished Dr. Wayland, then president of the university. After his graduation, in 1833, he entered the office of his brother in Providence with the intention of engaging with him in the business of manufacturing. He remained there five years, spending, however, a portion of his time in the prosecution of his business at Savannah, Georgia. At this time he was a casual contributor to newspapers and magazines, and a poem written by him during his stay in Savannah attracted considerable attention. We can readily imagine that he found literary work more congenial to his tastes than the exacting demands of a business life.

Mr. ANTHONY first became connected with public affairs as a journalist. In 1838, at the age of twenty-three, without previous training, except as an occasional contributor of literary articles, he assumed the editorial charge of the Providence Journal. He accepted the position at the request of a kinsman, who was then the proprietor of that paper, to fill a vacancy, and with the understanding that the arrangement was to continue only for a few weeks; but the connection thus made did not cease until the day of his death. His success as an editor was instant and marked. The time at which he took charge of the Journal was one of great political excitement in Rhode Island. The bitter struggle which was then going on to change the government of the State for the avowed purpose of securing an enlargement of the suffrage brought the contestants to the verge of civil war.

In this contest, Mr. ANTHONY, who, when a young man, as in later years, was conservative in his instincts, naturally took the side of "law and order." The triumph of the party to which he was attached was largely due to the vigorous and incisive advocacy of the Journal under his control. His brilliant leadership attracted some of the brightest and best men of his State to his support. The members of the party which he led with such consummate ability were prompt to acknowledge and to show their appreciation of the invaluable service which he rendered their cause. The conduct of the Journal in this controversy established Mr. ANTHONY'S reputation as a journalist, which then, and as long as he was actively engaged in the exercise of the profession, extended far beyond the limits of his own State. In the midst of a political contention of unsurpassed virulence he was never tempted by the impetuosity of youth nor driven by the malevolence of personal attacks, to write a sentence or utter a sentiment which would not bear the test of his maturer judgment, or which his friends would prefer should be erased or forgotten.

He was best known for the vigor and ability with which he wrote of political affairs, both State and national, and for his brilliant and genial satire; but the native dignity and courtesy of the man were manifested in the grace of style and ornate eloquence which distinguished all his literary workmanship. With a strong love for his profession, he had all the faculties of the ideal journalist—that of ready, clear, and forcible writing; of prompt decision in emergencies, combined with fair and temperate judgment; of wise choice in his associates and subordinates, with the cordial and friendly spirit of appreciation which secured their warm zeal and co-operation.

There was nothing labored in his work. He was an exceedingly rapid as well as an industrious writer, and has been known to keep four expert compositors busy in setting his manuscript. For years he performed the greater part of the editorial writing for the Journal, and even after his election to the Senate was for a long time in the habit of sending to the paper his daily contribution. To his latest day he kept up the habit of writing for its columns, and did not abandon it even under the pressure of enfeebling illness. His last paragraph, contributed a few days before his death, was a friendly notice of an acquaintance, and his last suggestion in its management was a request to spare a political enemy. The Journal was always the object of his affectionate care. His supervision of its columns was constant and close, and the suggestion that he should relieve himself of its responsibility, after the sudden death of his trusted associate, Mr. Danielson, under whose editorial management its reputation has been ably sustained and its sphere of usefulness enlarged, moved him to the expression that he would as soon think of parting with a child.

As a journalist Mr. ANTHONY was vigorous in controversy, and dealt in hard and sharp blows when he felt they were needed; but it was a characteristic of his temper as well as the secret of his success that he never indulged in unnecessary controversy or yielded to the temptation of being satirical merely for the sake of showing his skill. He never descended to abuse; and there was a kindly element in his keenest satire which robbed it of half its severity. His opponents always felt that they were dealing with an antagonist who would take no unfair advantage. His style of argument in the discussion of important subjects was remarkably clear and simple, and no one was ever at a loss to understand what he meant, or was at fault in following his train of thought.

In his later years he took special delight in writing on local topics in a spirit of genial humor and with all the graces of a true Addisonian style. His simple tributes to the memory of friends were marked with the same feeling eloquence which distinguished his elegiac orations in this Chamber. For many years Mr. ANTHONY was the Providence Journal. His individuality and his intellectual not less than his political influence made it the center of the intellectual life of Rhode Island, and attracted to it the contributions of the brightest minds in the State.

It is perhaps not too much to say that no paper in the country outside of the metropolitan journals had a higher reputation than the Providence Journal while Mr. ANTHONY was its editor, and that it was merely the limitation of its sphere that prevented him from being ranked in influence as a journalist with his great contemporaries of that remarkable era in American journalism. The volumes of the Journal while under his direction constitute his most conspicuous monument.

In 1849 Mr. ANTHONY was the nominee of the Whig party for governor of Rhode Island and was elected. His administration was successful, and he was re-elected in 1850, but declined a nomination for a third term.

Governor ANTHONY's position as a political leader in Rhode Island was then assured. The confidence of her people in his capacity and sagacity continued in a marked degree, and it was manifested in 1858 by his election to represent the State in the United States Senate. This office he assumed on the 4th of March, 1859, and by the uninterrupted favor and generous faith of his constituency, shown by five successive elections, he retained it for more than twenty-five years, until he was the oldest Senator in service and long after all his early associates had left this Chamber.

Entering the Senate in the full vigor of early manhood, he was splendidly equipped by nature and education, by a careful study of political history, and by an intimate knowledge of the science of government for the responsible duties of his high station. At this time the shadows of the approaching "irrepressible conflict" which was soon to involve the country in war had fallen upon the Capitol. Elected as a Republican, the first who was not openly allied with the Abolitionists, his conservative tendencies did not prevent his taking the earliest opportunity to attest his devotion to the cause of liberty.

To recount the events in which Senator ANTHONY during the years of his service was a participant, or of which he was a witness, would be to recite the history of the country for its most interesting and important period. I cannot, however, forbear an allusion to his valuable services during the critical years of the late civil war. In this momentous crisis he brought to the discharge of his important duties in the Senate, and as a trusted counselor of the Executive, great good sense, sound nerves, a clear, cool judgment, a courage never dismayed by disaster, and a loyalty and patriotism equal to any sacrifice or emergency. We have, as a people, justly bestowed our highest honors upon the military heroes who at that time rendered conspicuous service to the country, but it may be doubted whether we have properly estimated the influence and services of those who in the national councils shared the responsibility of the great contest.

Measured by the length of time employed, Senator AN-THONY's greatest labors while a member of this body were on the Committee on Public Printing, of which he was the chairman for more than twenty-two years. During this period, and largely through his influence, the extravagant and corrupt system of contract printing was abolished, a national printing office established, the publication of debates transferred from private hands to the Public Printer, and economical reforms in the manner of purchasing paper and other supplies were initiated. He sought, unsuccessfully, to restrict the public printing to the legitimate demands of the various governmental departments, and to prevent the publication for popular distribution of large and expensive editions of works of questionable value. He also endeavored, with equal lack of success, to make the Congressional Record what it purports to be, a faithful transcript of Congressional proceedings, and to prevent its "leaden columns" from being weighed down by the insertion of speeches which were never spoken.

Senator ANTHONY served from 1863 to his death on the Committee on Naval Affairs, of which he was for many years the senior member. He was familiar with the condition and wants of the Navy, and was greatly interested in promoting all measures which promised to add to its efficiency. Meritorious officers always found in him an earnest advocate and firm friend.

Senator ANTHONY was elected President *pro tempore* of this body in March, 1863, and re-elected in March, 1871, serving for four years. In this position he displayed rare abilities as a parliamentarian and presided over the Senate with grace and dignity. In January, 1884, he was again elected, but, "with a heart overflowing with gratitude," felt obliged to decline, as the state of his health warned him not to assume any labors that he could honorably avoid.

Senator ANTHONY never consumed the time of the Senate in useless discussion, but on the rare occasions when he participated in debate his remarks were characterized by both clearness of statement and soundness of argument. His memorial addresses, in which he rendered graceful and grateful tribute to the memory of departed Senators, are accepted as models of perfect taste, and are marked by an elegance of style and a spirit of kindly but just criticism which command universal admiration. Ranking with these in grace of style are his address at the completion of the equestrian statue of General Greene near the Capitol, which owes its existence to his exertions; his speeches on the occasion of the presentation by the State of Rhode Island to the National Government of the statues of Roger Williams and General Greene, and his remarks in favor of an appropriation for the restoration of the monument which marks the last resting-place of the Chevalier De Ternay, at Newport.

As a Senator he applied himself steadfastly to the absorbing duties which crowd a senatorial life, never neglecting any appeal or demand from his constituents. No man had a more exalted idea of the dignity and importance of the senatorial office than he ; and none was more careful to preserve intact its time-honored privileges and prerogatives. He was inflexibly opposed to all innovations on established precedents in modes of procedure, and was accepted as authority on all matters pertaining to senatorial etiquette. He held a position of honorable and commanding influence among his associates in the Senate and in the councils of his party.

He was by nature incapable of doing a mean act. With a high sense of political and personal honor, no narrow influences ever controlled his political action. Living at a time when few reputations escaped attack, it is a matter for congratulation that his long public career closed without a stain upon his honor and without the breath of suspicion resting on any of his official acts. Neither foes nor rivals ever ventured to question his uprightness or his strict integrity.

Senator ANTHONY was a devoted son of Rhode Island, proud of her institutions, fond of her traditions, and familiar with every phase of her not unglorious history. With uncommon solicitude he had watched her wonderful industrial growth and intellectual development. For half a century he had been more influential than any other of her citizens in molding public sentiment and directing the policy of her people; and as the acknowledged leader of the dominant party in the State, his influence in political matters was, for a large portion of this time, controlling. He implanted and nurtured a patriotic spirit in the hearts of her sons, which will continue to bear fruit in perpetual remembrance of his example.

In every forum and on every occasion, whenever her institutions were assailed or any principle dear to her people brought in question, he became her advocate and defender, using every weapon of offensive or defensive warfare with all the skill of a veteran and all the enthusiastic ardor of a youthful recruit. He was impelled to this service rather by the promptings of affection than the demands of duty. This engrossing love for his native State was his grand passion, and to serve her interests with fidelity was the one undeviating purpose of his life, dominating all circumstances and surroundings. He never, however, found his intense loyalty to his State in conflict with his duty as a Senator of the United States.

His exceptional success as a political leader, in a community where many ambitious and able men were disposed to dispute his ascendency, did not depend alone upon that esteem and confidence of his fellow-citizens which is the natural reward for devoted services. He had the faculty of forming a correct judgment of the character and capacity of those with whom he came in contact, and there was a subtle charm in his nature

which appealed strongly to the sensibilities of others, attracting
men of the most diverse characteristics and attaching them
firmly to himself and his fortunes.   His manner was always
conciliatory; his temper was never impulsive, and his persist-
ence rarely assumed an aggressive form.   He persuaded and
prevailed more by the moderation of his spirit than by the
vigor and comprehensiveness of his understanding.   He was
faithful to his friends, clinging fondly to old companions and
associations; but this did not prevent his prompt recognition
and appreciation of the new men, with special qualities for
leadership, whom changing circumstances brought into prominence.

He was a zealous party man, but he never used the patronage
or power of official station to advance his personal interests.
When required to decide, as he often was, upon the compara-
tive merit of aspirants for political preferment, he invariably
made fitness and a capacity to advance the public welfare, the
only standard of judgment.

His associates here can hardly fail to speak with warmth of
his striking personal characteristics; of the genial and gracious
presence—in manner and essence that of a gentleman—which
has so long adorned this Chamber.   Here he was faithful in
his attachments, tolerant of his opponents; and the unusual
sweetness and uniformity of his temper endeared him to all
with whom he came in contact.   He never practiced the arts
of the demagogue, but he had a strong attraction for all that
was real, genuine, and manly, and an instinctive dislike for
shams and everything like cant or hypocrisy.   He detested
display and pretension, and shrank from notoriety.   He had
an inexhaustible fund of human gentleness, which made him
naturally courteous and amiable; but his courtesy and polite-

ness never offended by taking the form of condescension. He was considerate of the feelings and comfort of others; quick to discover and commend merit. His nature was cast in finest mold—

> His life was gentle, and the elements
> So mix'd in him, that Nature might stand up
> And say to all the world, This was a man!

He was a strong man mentally and physically, but no disproportion marred the symmetry of his character, and no irregular outlines called attention to the strength and beauty of the structure.

His conversation abounded in simple and delightful charms, and he was a favorite in every social circle. His hospitality had all the elegance of that of a gentleman of the old school, and his house in Providence was always the attractive center of a circle of brilliant men and women.

It was painfully evident when Senator ANTHONY last attended the sessions of the Senate that death had marked him for its victim; and no one knew this better than himself, for he had been informed by his physician as early as April, 1883, of the fatal character of the disease from which he was suffering. Returning to his home in April last, he proceeded with perfect composure to set his house in order for the great change. During the months which followed he awaited the dread summons with a patience and philosophic calmness which deeply impressed all those who were about him. With the slow wasting of his physical powers there was no visible impairment of his mental faculties. The letters written by his own hand during this period had all the peculiar grace and charm of style which made him master of the epistolary art.

He was singularly reticent even to his most intimate friends in regard to his inner being, but whenever the uncertain tenure of his life was mentioned he always manifested a spirit of humble submission to Divine will, and would say, "God's time is best." In the face of death his courage never faltered; and the lessons of faith which had been taught him by a Christian mother were never forgotten. "He had," to use the words of his friend, Rev. Mr. Woodbury, in his eloquent funeral discourse, "schooled himself to that serenity of soul which could not be disturbed either in life or death." At his home devoted friends and relatives ministered to his comfort, and the ablest medical skill sought by the use of every remedy known to science to stay the progress of the disease, but all their efforts were in vain. On the 2d of September last he peacefully sank to rest. He was buried from the neighboring church where the funeral rites of his beloved colleague, General Burnside, had been so recently solemnized. "Twin heirs of fame," their precious dust reposes in the same cemetery, and their memories are together graven on the hearts of the people of Rhode Island.

His funeral, without pageantry or display, was an appropriate tribute of honor to the distinguished dead. It was attended by the President of the United States, a large number of Senators, and the official representatives of his State and city.

In the history of the Senate others have served as faithfully and as honorably as he whom we mourn, but it is rare that length of service unite with a high order of intellect and a spotless reputation to form a senatorial career as impressive, as instructive, and as patriotic as that which is now closed in the grave of HENRY B. ANTHONY.

Remarks by Mr. EDMUNDS, of Vermont.

Again, Mr. President, we pause in our consideration of measures affecting the material welfare of millions of living beings and give the hour to our recollections of our departed friend and associate, and to lay upon his tomb our glad tributes to his worth and our sad memories of his loss to his friends and his countrymen.

Scenes like this, common as they are, never over the wide world lose their interest. Infidel, and pagan, and Christian alike celebrate them, and in varying forms and with differing hopes and aspirations come to weep over the graves of their fellow-men. To all alike the veil that separates the present of life from its future is equally impenetrable to the natural eye; but to the eye of faith and hope, and, as I think, to the philosophic vision as well, there opens a field of view which should lead us not to mourn at the death in the fullness of accomplished years of those we have loved and respected, but rather to be soberly glad for them, who, having faithfully filled their space and appointed time and having borne the last trial of humanity, have been admitted to the life of the mysterious future. We see "through a glass darkly," indeed, but our friend and all who have gone before and with him do, I believe, see and feel clearly the peace that belongs to them who with pure hearts and faithful endeavor have, in whatever station, run the race that was set before them.

The almost twenty years of close intimacy with which Mr. ANTHONY honored me filled me more and more, as time went on, with admiration of his character and with strong personal affection. A gentleman of more perfect honor and of more perfect kindness of heart, of more catholicity of spirit, of less bigotry, of less envy or uncharitableness, or of less self-seeking I have never known. So knowing him, I could not choose but love him.

> He never made a brow look dark,
> Nor caused a tear but when he died.

His public life was one embracing a period of events as stupendous and important as any that can occur in the history of nations. Through it all in the respects I have mentioned he was almost peerless among his peers. His close associates were among the pillars of the nation's fortune. Many of them have gone to their reward before him. There were Sumner, and Wilson, and Collamer, and Foot, and Johnson, and Wade, and Fessenden, and Chandler, and Howard, and Grimes, and Howe—these were they who chiefly in the Senate carried the nation triumphantly through its great struggle and restored it to its broad foundations with the bright, new corner-stone of liberty, and they honored him in his place in his party and in the Senate, as I now do his gracious memory, as with a constant benediction.

Strongly devoted to his party, he yet always stood for the liberty of individual senatorial opinion and action, and in all conferences, when needful, he reminded his colleagues of the rule of his party in the Senate that preserves to each Senator the full liberty to follow his honest convictions without reproach from his fellows. He desired unity of action, but he desired still more to "follow right because right *is* right in scorn of consequence." He could not believe that "dissimulation in political action was to be regarded as a public virtue, or that when men asserted the dignity of truth their candor was to be charged against them as a heinous crime." In all the long trials of the war and in all the time of the difficulties and bitterness that followed it I have never heard that he had wounded the feelings or incurred the resentment of any gentleman of either party in the Senate. In all contests and disputes his gentleness of feeling and manner and his strict observance of every courtesy in debate compelled the sympathy and good-will of his opponents, if they did not secure their adhesion to his views.

As a speaker his voice was clear and sweet, but his real diffidence of himself and his fear of consuming time sometimes produced a faulty and too rapid utterance. As a writer he had marked excellence, and in some departments of composition his writings have seemed to me as perfect as any in the English language with which I am acquainted.

The same qualities of mind and heart to which I have alluded made him a favorite in the wide social circles of the capital. He was everywhere a welcome visitor. He was neither scandal-monger nor tale-bearer. He never indulged in coarseness or vulgarity, but his conversation ran pleasantly along on topics of history, biography, anecdote, and poetry, for which last he had a particular fondness. I have often heard him repeat favorite passages with a tenderness of feeling and a grace of expression that showed how perfectly he sympathized with the inmost sentiment of the writer.

As he has here so often done for the memory of his departed friends, we now make our last formal memorial of him. In the years that are to come I can only hope for our country that all her Senators may have his fidelity and worth, and that those

who hereafter celebrate similar occasions in the Senate may
be able to speak as truly and kindly of the departed as we now
do of him.

> He leaves behind him, freed from grief and years,
> Far worthier things than tears,
> The love of friends without a single foe:
> Unequaled lot below!

Remarks by Mr. BAYARD, of Delaware.

Mr. PRESIDENT: The list has grown to be long indeed which
records the deaths of those who have been my associates in this
Chamber, and among them all, the living as well as the dead, I
know not one more sedulous, considerate, and impressive in the
payment of the last marks of sorrowing respect and brother-
hood to his deceased associates than the worthy gentleman
whose death induces these remarks.

To "weep with them that weep" was an injunction little
needed by Mr. ANTHONY, whose kindly and sympathetic nature found frequent, eloquent, and admirable expression in the
elegiac addresses delivered by him in the Senate as one after
another his friends and associates passed in melancholy procession before him to the tomb. And now, at last, he also, ripe
in years and wisdom, has been gathered in the harvest of mor-
tality by the inevitable hand of the grim reaper.

As a Senator from the State of Rhode Island Mr. ANTHONY
sat in this council chamber for nearly twenty-six years, and
seldom has any one served so long and so worthily.

Without the wish or probably the faculty to impress himself
as a leader among men, yet he was recognized and sought by
those who were and are leaders as a wise and safe counselor.
While not participating frequently in debate, few were so intel-

ligently observant of the course of public business or wiser or juster in their judgments respecting it.

As a parliamentarian Mr. ANTHONY excelled, and elected, as he frequently was, to be the President *pro tempore* of the body, his skill in parliamentary law and procedure and in the dispatch of business, accompanied by unfailing courtesy and impartiality, gave him a hold upon the respect of all parties that always remained unbroken.

The spirit of comity, courtesy, and thoughtful consideration of others animated him and marked his conduct in the performance of his duties in this Chamber; and while we who were the beneficiaries of these admirable qualities felt our indebtedness, there can be no doubt that his usefulness and capability as a representative to render successful and important services to his constituents was in turn greatly increased.

Mr. ANTHONY was strict and tenacious as a party man, and was largely controlled here by his party allegiance, but I never knew it to take the form of offense or imputation of a political opponent, and I may truly say that in sixteen years of association here I never saw his face darkened by a frown, much less disfigured by a sneer.

A touching and impressive instance of the feeling he had inspired among his associates was afforded when, at the commencement of his fifth term of senatorial service, as he advanced to take the constitutional oath, the entire Senate rose and remained standing during its administration.

I knew him well, and relations of steady friendliness subsisted between us, unbroken by differences of opinion and political association, and it was as a sincere mourner that I followed his body to its last resting-place, in the State of his nativity which he had served so long and well.

We had been sorrowful witnesses here of the gradual decline in his health for several years, and the final summons was not unexpected by him nor by those who surrounded him.

In the death of Mr. ANTHONY the United States have lost one of their most experienced and respected public servants, the State of Rhode Island a distinguished, valued, and faithful representative, and every member of this Senate a genial and well-beloved friend.

Remarks by Mr. PENDLETON, of Ohio.

Mr. PRESIDENT: I bring my tribute of respect and affection for our dead brother.

Senators who had the pleasure of long association with him in this body, and that intimate acquaintance which the public and private proceedings of the Senate seem always to promote, have done and others still will do justice to his life and character, to his qualities of head and heart, to his principles and methods. Although not always in the association of the Senate Chamber, I knew Senator ANTHONY long and well.

When he came to the Senate I was a member of the House of Representatives. The stirring events which soon followed in 1860-'61 brought us into contact. The differences of our party associations and modes of thought as to the impending struggle were very great. They did not divide us; indeed, they seemed to bind us closer together, so soon as we fully understood that each of us honestly cherished and faithfully supported a common purpose to preserve by whatever variant methods an "indissoluble Union of indestructible States."

I soon learned to know how decided were his convictions, how resolute his assertion of them, how unbending his will in carrying them into execution. And yet how courteous his manners and gentle his judgment of opinions and actions differing from his own! I soon learned to appreciate those genial qualities of temper and manner which soften the asperities of thought and action dealing with the fate of nations in flagrant civil war.

Time passed. Our intercourse as members of Congress ceased. A most agreeable companionship followed, when for many years the heats of long, exhaustive summers were escaped in the delights of an unequaled climate at Newport, or on the shores of his native Narraganset. There he threw off the cares of public life, the harness of party, and was the genial, friendly, cultivated, agreeable gentleman, administering to the enjoyment of many friends who gathered in that most favored region of Rhode Island.

Again we met as members of this body. The favor of our respective party friends assigned us corresponding positions in our party conferences; and then I came to know him still better. His fidelity to party obligation was inflexible and pronounced. His appreciation of a like fidelity among his opponents, his candor, and suavity, and honor were equally conspicuous.

His intellect was strong; his information was large; his culture was wide and generous; his views of public duty were fixed; his aims were lofty; his methods were honorable; his heart was true and kind; his courtesy never failed. I think he never willingly wounded the feelings of any one. He was faithful and wise as a committeeman. He was fully conversant with the current business of the Senate. He was an admirable presiding officer; the very master—*facile princeps*—in all questions of ceremonial and dignified propriety.

The little volume of addresses in which Senator ANTHONY commemorated the qualities of his friends who had died in the Senate testifies to the truth of all I have said.

The style is rich but simple. The taste is faultless. The fountain of sympathetic appreciation is exhaustless. The judgment is just but kindly. The philosophy is of that calm and patient and hopeful faith in which he was born. "There is One that doeth all things well" was the pervading thought as the great dead fell around him. Even as early as 1874, "musing on the transitory nature of all sublunary things," he recalls with touching pathos that since his entrance to this Chamber every other seat save one had changed its occupant and into the vacant places had stepped others, who had put on the armor which those who had gone before had worn, lifted the weapons which they had wielded, and marched to the work which they had inaugurated.

And thus—

He exclaimed—

I am filled with reverent wonder at the beneficent ordering of nature, and inspired with a loftier faith in that almighty Power without whose guidance and direction all human effort is vain, and with whose blessing the humblest instruments He selects are equal to the mightiest work that He designs.

For twenty-five years he served well his State; and with faculties unimpaired, with the duties of life discharged, the trusts of life fulfilled, died at the age allowed by the wisdom of God and the experience of man as the most fortunate for translation to other spheres of existence and duty; even to the last the recipient of the highest honors, political and social, which the respect and confidence and affection of its citizens could confer.

In his own language I repeat:

To complain at the close of such a life is to complain that the ripened fruit drops from the overloaded bough, that the golden harvest bends to the sickle; it is to complain of the law of our existence, and to accuse the Creator that He did not make man immortal on the earth.

To him the wondrous portals of the unseen world have opened; and perhaps the mysteries of death, revealing, "what was and is and is to come," have solved the mysteries of life. Faith may disclose to our grateful eyes glimpses of heaven's beatitudes, yet when his associates here realize that we shall see his face again no more forever "one human tear shall fall and be forgiven."

Remarks by Mr. MORRILL, of Vermont.

Mr. PRESIDENT: Called, as we so often are, to lament the departure of one of our fellow-members, we are prone to feel the lesson less bitter from its frequent recurrence and forget it as "a tale that is told;" but the prominence here of the late Senator ANTHONY, for a quarter of a century of continuous service, lends to the present occasion exceptional interest. To me, his senior in age, and attached to him by all the ligaments which bind associates in public and private life, the event brings a message of admonition peculiarly impressive. In the common course of nature the scene would have been reversed and my labors should have earliest ended, while he should now be here. Truly "we know not what a day may bring forth." Almost from my first entrance to the Senate it was my good fortune to sit by the side of him whose decease we now mourn, and it is almost unnecessary to say that I found my near neighbor not only a delightful talker but a patient listener, and his

occasional wayside conversation, with its full flow of spirits and
store of anecdote, indulged in tones not drowning senatorial
debate, made his presence welcome by the same abounding
attractions which everywhere made him so general a favorite
in society. His empty chair proclaims the Senate's loss, and I
feel sure many longing hearts are ready with me to exclaim:

> O for the touch of a vanished hand,
> And the sound of a voice that is still.

HENRY B. ANTHONY was a man beloved. His character, as
well as his person, was attractive, and his bearing manly.
Even those who chanced to differ with him in opinion found
nothing repulsive in his manner. His ambition was fully satisfied with being an American Senator, and, having befitting
intellectual tastes and aptitudes, having a high ideal standard
for the service, he was careful to maintain the prestige and to
preserve the traditions and prerogatives of the Senate. He was
familiar with all of its parliamentary usages and forms, and
the proprieties of its proceedings, when guided by him, lost
nothing of grace and dignity. As the President *pro tempore* of
the Senate he was thoroughly the master of the rules, wholly
impartial, and largely contributed to the correct and brisk dispatch of business. His handiwork, known as "the Anthony
rule," is likely to be long approved as a method of forwarding
the daily work of the Senate. In the chair, as everywhere, he
was a ready man. His mind moved with the same electric
swiftness that characterized his spoken words. Questions of
order did not hang fire, and from his prompt decisions an
appeal was seldom or never taken.

As the chairman of the Joint Committee on Printing, the
late Senator, from his practical knowledge, exercised a constant and commanding influence, and, though not always able

to restrain the vote to print documents—the value of which often disappears with the revolving year—within the limits he judged proper, yet his conservative action was ever deeply rooted in the line of economy. The art of printing he esteemed as really the "art preservative of all arts," and he had some pride in having Government printing done by the Government, and better done than it could be elsewhere. This he believed to have been successfully accomplished, and we are indebted to the late chairman as the promoter of many improvements, until at length, more or less under his promptings, the Government commands the skill and machinery to produce work in the foremost style of typography.

The services of Senator ANTHONY upon the Committee on Naval Affairs were long and conspicuous. With the exception of the late Senator Grimes, of Iowa, whose mastery of all naval matters was simply marvelous, I think he had a more precise and thorough knowledge of every vessel and of every officer of the Navy than any person not officially connected with its service. He was proud of the "old sea dogs" and of their heroic exploits. He could name those competent to command a fleet or a squadron, or those whose genius and blood could be trusted to conduct a naval battle, and he looked upon a proper navy in a large measure as the custodian of the national honor, as well as the chief if not all-sufficient arm of national defense. He was alert in guarding the high reputation of the *personnel* of the Navy, or in keeping it clear of epauletted barnacles, and no officer, when dismissed from the service for worshiping Bacchus instead of Neptune, ever had a fresh opportunity to lose a ship or the lives of men by being restored to place through his aid. He was full of reverence for our national flag, and to his eye the starry banner, when waving from "the mast of some great ammiral," appeared in its highest splendor.

Senator ANTHONY did not often venture upon *extempore* speaking, though upon emergencies he appeared to lack neither fluency nor effectiveness; but his prepared speeches were marked by abundant research, vigor of thought, and were clothed with all the graces of classical culture. His speech in defense of some peculiar features of the constitution of his native State, inherited from its colonial origin, displayed the full forces of his learning, logic, and loyalty, and Rhode Island will look in vain for a defender more intrepid or better equipped.

His memorial addresses, of which years ago he reprinted a collated edition, were models of beauty and pathos. Few more impressive and appropriate tributes to deceased associates will be found in the records of the Senate than the felicitous eulogiums pronounced here by him whose long and honorable career has just closed, and whose decease brings us all together here as a band of brothers. His discourses on these sad occasions sometimes seemed to me almost to rob death of its terrors, and that, heralded to the "unseen world" covered by his gracious mantle of testimonials, one would "even dare to die." These utterances were the throbbings of a generous heart, eloquently and conscientiously spoken, and delicately perfumed. Thinking no evil, and incapable of malice, he could not have a "sterile admiration" for his friends, and when he bid them an everlasting farewell he did not fail to decorate them with *immortelles.*

His brief address to the governor of Massachusetts, as chairman of the committee accompanying the remains of Charles

Sumner, was worthy of the "illustrious dead," and will live as a happy specimen of spontaneous and genuine eloquence.

The late Senator ANTHONY was void of all conceit; did not "think of himself more highly than he ought to think;" never attempted to offer instruction upon questions he had not fully studied; and never pretended to that intuitive genius which comprehends all subjects, but he aimed to do thoroughly well the work that fell to his lot. Without surrendering cardinal principles, he was outspoken and generous in his appreciation of the merits of others, whether they were arrayed on this side of the Chamber or the other. Though affectionately attached to his friends, no asperities of political life invaded his personal or social relations. Eloquence in the Senate or a great debate, equally with the foremost examples of ancient history, lingered long in his memory, and was accounted by him as an appropriate and enduring contribution to the renown of his country.

Senator ANTHONY was one of the proprietors, and for many years the chief editor, of the Providence Journal, the leading Republican paper of Rhode Island, with an enviable reputation throughout the country. The editorials of the Journal were bright and scholarly, but, somewhat like those of Thurlow Weed, George D. Prentice, and Horace Greeley, generally rather short, and noted, as well as extensively copied, for their sterling good sense. The editorial profession, which he so early adorned, did not fail to tincture his later career, nor fail to largely contribute to his public usefulness. In his copartner, Mr. Danielson, so long as he lived, he found also a gifted and most valuable editorial associate, and the Journal securely maintained its position as one of the most prosperous and influential papers in New England.

As a man he never seemed to be deserted by his good genius, and never to do or say a foolish thing. All of his speeches, therefore, were scarcely less than models of good taste. They were never dull, but always crisp and without redundant words. His calm judgment, undisturbed by crotchets, together with his transparent sincerity, gave to his opinions positive weight, and to any discussion where he was a participant he brought visible and valuable contributions.

He was in the first year of his fifth term of service in the Senate. This remarkably protracted distinction emphasized the abiding confidence and affection of the people of his State, and was in harmony with the almost equal love and respect of the people of the country at large. It will not be too much to say that it was thoroughly merited by his high-toned integrity, by his conceded ability, and by his unselfish devotion to every public duty. Throughout the long and historic career of this distinguished son of Rhode Island, who here survived all of his early associates, the world has ever recognized the bearing and just proportions of an American Senator, and virtues most worthy of imitation. He leaves us without a word he could wish to blot. He leaves us with the completed record of a useful and blameless life. He faithfully bore his part in the Senate during an era of great national events, and history will lovingly guard his memory.

— —

Remarks by Mr. GARLAND, of Arkansas.

Mr. PRESIDENT: In the accurate sketch of the life and character of Senator ANTHONY just now presented by his former colleague on this floor we have a beautiful picture of a life noiseless and of even tenor, but industrious and laborious, devoted to good private acts and great public service, and a character simple, amiable, affectionate, yet commanding.

Educated for that most jealous and exacting of all professions, the law, his health failing, he embarked in the business of newspaper editing. In this broad field of influence and of usefulness, in which so many of the first men of our country have figured, he maintained, as he did in all things he undertook, a high and prominent rank. From this sphere he went to the governorship of his State, where he served her so well and so faithfully she became not merely attached to him, but devoted to him, from that time till he was laid away for the long sleep in the dark chamber, in her own bosom.

Coming to this body as her Senator in 1859, when such men as Fessenden, Douglas, Seward, Hunter, Sumner, Toombs, Trumbull, Jefferson Davis, Crittenden, and Benjamin were honored members of this Chamber, he soon took rank with them as a most able and valuable colaborer. Elected for five consecutive terms, he rendered longer unbroken service here than any Senator in our history save Mr. Benton, of Missouri. Mr. King, of Alabama, served longer, but his terms were not continuous, while Mr. Sumner had twenty-three years of consecutive service.

While this compliment is so rare, in this case it was well merited, for Mr. ANTHONY was industrious in his senatorial work, well instructed in all its details, and faithful to the last.

He rarely engaged in what are called purely political debates, but when he did he showed he was equal to the demands of the occasion.

His speeches, made generally with a view of throwing light on questions of public policy and aiding in their solution, were plain and simple in their style—"neither affected nor elaborate, and remarkable for the absence of all words of questionable authority."

Well versed in parliamentary law, he was a stickler for the enforcement of the rules of the Senate as a means for the preservation of order and the transaction of business; and his usefulness in this way was on several occasions fully recognized by his brother Senators in their selection of him to preside over the deliberations of this body.

Almost from the time I began to take an interest in Congressional proceedings Mr. ANTHONY was a well-known and distinguished actor in them. From then till very recently, to read these deliberations was to become somewhat familiar with him. Eight years ago, when I became a member of the Senate, he was here, conspicuous and leading, and was then, except for the presence of the venerable Hamlin, the father of the Senate, as he was so affectionately called by his brothers here in the latter days of his service. To me, therefore, the Senate seems unnatural without him; it is most difficult to realize his absence, and by us all and the country his loss is deeply deplored.

His conduct in life was without parade or ostentation. Without pretensions, his movements and acts spoke for themselves, a full exemplification of what Sallust said of Cato: *Esse, quam videri.*

His manners were attractive to the last degree to those who associated with him, and to be thrown with him was to sincerely admire him.

He merited by his public works and by his private virtues the respect and affection of his countrymen, and the best wish for his country and his office is that his mantle may fall upon his successor.

Remarks by Mr. HOAR, of Massachusetts.

Mr. PRESIDENT: In paying the tribute of the Senate to our senior, the eminent Senator from Rhode Island, it is fitting that his State and those who were nearest to him in friendship and in length of service should have been first heard. But it would be unjust to Massachusetts if her profound sympathy with her neighbor and her own sense of public loss did not also find expression. No two States in the Union are bound together by closer ties than Massachusetts and Rhode Island. Their affection was never broken. When Roger Williams went out to lay for the first time in human history the foundation of a State in religious liberty, he retained, undiminished, his love for the people he had left behind. He earnestly desired that the younger Winthrop should become the governor of his infant Commonwealth. From that day to this the occasions have been few and unimportant and temporary in which there has been any considerable difference of opinion between these sister States. Their character, their interests, their employments have been the same. Together their soldiers and sailors met danger and victory under Perry and Greene, the illustrious captains of Rhode Island. William Ellery Channing, who, beyond all other men, has influenced the character of Massachusetts in later times, was the gift to her of Rhode Island. When the whole structure of her civil society was in danger, Rhode Island sought and found her successful champion in Daniel Webster. There were no sincerer mourners at the grave of Burnside than the citizen soldiers of Massachusetts. No voice spoke the universal sorrow for the death of Sumner more affectionately and tenderly than that we miss to-day.

Mr. Anthony, after having been twice governor of his own State, was five times chosen to the Senate for a full term. If his life had been spared, he would have had a longer period of unbroken service here than any other person since the Senate was organized. Owing to the delay in the admission of Missouri, Mr. Benton was not elected until late in 1821. His first term ended March 4, 1827. Mr. Anthony served in the Senate, in fact, longer than any other person, except Mr. Benton.

I think we may offer him to the judgment of history as the model of the character of the Senator as our fathers conceived it. Superior, by the length of his constitutional term of office, and by his own personal weight, to what is fluctuating and temporary in the popular sentiment of his State, yet representing what is best and most permanent in its character and opinion— member of a body whose organization has continued and is to continue without a break from the time the Constitution was inaugurated until it shall perish, the never broken chain binding the remote past to the far remoter future—the Senator alone, as his name implies, stands for the principle of seniority in the Republic. Mr. Anthony was the depositary of the unwritten traditions of this body. He never failed to maintain, so far as in him lay, its authority and dignity. He had a wide circle of friends, and was above all others the one most welcome guest in the hospitable circles of Washington. But his only home was the Senate Chamber. It cannot be doubted that he was thinking of his own lot when he uttered that touching passage in his eulogy on Wilson:

Home he had none. No man shared more largely in the affections of the American people; no man was more beloved by his immediate constituency; but those pleasures which the greatest of American orators placed above all the other immeasurable blessings of rational existence, above the treasures of science and the delights of learning and the aspects of nature, even above good government and religious liberty, "the transcendent sweets of domestic life," were no more for him. Those relations which nature intended for the joy and the rapture of our youth, for the happiness and the embellishment of our maturer years, for the comfort and consolation of age, had been severed by the remorseless shears of fate. No eye grew brighter when he raised the latch that held his lonely dwelling; no outstretched arms of wife, no ringing laughter of children, welcomed his returning footsteps, when he crossed the threshold over which all that had given life, and joy, and beauty to that simple abode, and had lighted it up with a glory not of palaces, had been borne never to return. He had nothing left to love but his country.

He was fully able to defend himself and his State and any cause which he espoused. No man would attack either with impunity under circumstances which called on him for reply, as he showed on some memorable occasions. But he was of a most gracious and sweet nature. He was a lover and maker of peace. When an indignity was by his own political associates put upon the great leader of emancipation in the Senate which had been the scene of his illustrious service, no man regretted the occurrence more than Mr. Anthony.

> And straight Patroclus rose,
> The genial comrade, who, amid the strife
> Of kings, and war of angry utterance,
> Held even balance, to his outraged friend
> Heart-true, yet ever strove with kindly words
> To hush the jarring discord, urging peace.

Mr. Anthony was a learned man; learned in the history of the Senate and in parliamentary law; learned in the history of his country and of foreign countries; learned in the resources of a full, accurate, and graceful scholarship. Since Sumner died I suppose none of us can be compared with him in this respect. Some passages in an almost forgotten political satire show that he possessed a vein which, if he had cultivated it,

might have placed him high in the roll of satiric poets. But
he never launched a shaft that he might inflict a sting. His
collection of memorial addresses is unsurpassed in its kind of
literature. He was absolutely simple, modest, courteous, and
without pretense. He was content to do his share in accom-
plishing public results, and to leave to others whatever of fame
or glory might result from having accomplished them.

> To be, and not to seem, was this man's wisdom.

Gentle and kindly in his judgments, he could be firm and
stern when public duty required. He steadfastly resisted
everything which seemed to him to relax the discipline or
lower the standard of character in the Navy to whose glory
his State has so largely contributed.

He was fortunate in life. He lived and took a great part in
great historic events in a great age. His senatorial service
corresponded almost exactly with the term of power enjoyed
by the great party to which he belonged. He saw the beginning and the final triumph of the political movement to
which a race, that, within two generations, will number more
than thirty millions in this country, owes its emancipation.
He had his full share in advising and framing the measures
by which rebellion was subdued and his country saved. He
had his full share, also, in that great self-control by which the
restored nation manifested alike its unparalleled clemency and
its unparalleled integrity, greater in ruling its own spirit than
in conquering states or taking cities. Through all this, I cannot think of an utterance he would wish to blot or a vote he
would desire to recall. *Recte, te Cyre, beatum ferunt, quoniam
virtuti tuæ fortuna conjuncta est.*

He was fortunate also in death. He escaped that sudden
and unprepared parting against which the church offers her

prayers. He escaped, also, the weakness and decay of age. Death came to him without pain and without a shock, while his intellectual forces were unimpaired. His life had been stainless, honored, useful, happy. He was beloved by his associates here, beloved by the people of the State of which he was the citizen first in honor and in station, beloved by his whole reunited country.

The great orator and philosopher of Rome declared in his youth, and repeated in his age, that death could not come prematurely to a man who had been consul. Cicero spake to a senate to whom Christianity was unknown and immortality but a dream. Surely we cannot mourn as untimely the ending of the life of a man who has been five times Senator. To us, to whom Christianity holds out its promise of an existence continued somewhere, where the virtues developed here shall continue and grow, it is matter of high exultation that a soul so pure, so lofty, so fortunate, has passed on safely, and without a stain, to another stage of being, where

> that, which lived
> True life, lives on.

Remarks by Mr. BUTLER, of South Carolina.

Mr. PRESIDENT: My friendly regard and high respect for Governor ANTHONY began soon after I became a member of this body and continued uninterruptedly to his death. Though one of the oldest veterans in the service, and many years my senior, he was nevertheless accessible at all times to younger men, and invariably courteous and kindly. His personal qualities were so attractive that we were instinctively drawn to him. His equanimity of temper, amiability of disposition, dignified and affable demeanor, and cordial social virtues were uniform and almost exceptional, so that he was always a welcome guest in social life, a genial, companionable gentleman.

Simple, unaffected, unpretending in his professions, he was a most faithful, trustworthy, and devoted friend. We all remember how devotedly attached he was to his life-long friend and colleague, General Burnside; how devotedly this attachment was reciprocated, and what a touching eulogy he pronounced upon that friend in this Chamber. During my term of service here with Governor ANTHONY we have passed through some of the most exciting, acrimonious debates ever known in the Senate, and yet I do not remember that one expression of bitterness or one word of personal reproach toward his political opponents ever escaped his lips. This is a great deal to be said of any man, Mr. President, who has passed through such trying ordeals and irritating scenes, but I am sure every one of his brethren of this body will bear me out and that it is sustained by the record. I can pronounce no higher encomium upon his character as a Senator and gentleman. His mental qualities and intellectual attainments were as marked and high as his personal attractions. In a word, sir, his whole make-up, moral, mental, intellectual, and physical, was as completely rounded off with uniform symmetry as any man I have ever known. As gentle and kindly in his sympathies as a woman, he was nevertheless as stern, as earnest, and unyielding in the discharge of what he conceived to be his duty as the most robust nature.

Our party affiliations and associations threw us on opposing political lines; and while he was regarded by his political opponents as a staunch and faithful adherent to the party of his faith, his partisanship never became so intense or unreasonable as to become offensive to those who differed with him or to forfeit their personal regard. I do not think that Governor Anthony, in a popular sense, could have been considered a party leader. His mental and intellectual organization rather led him to the literary and scholarly side of politics. And yet it was generally understood by those of us not in the councils of his party that in consultation his judgment exercised a commanding influence in determining party policy. In questions before the Senate of a non-partisan character, in the conduct of business, in the real work of legislation, his well-earned experience, faithful, conscientious attention to the duties of his high station, carried great weight with his brother Senators of all parties.

He rarely participated in general debate, but was always at his post of duty, and when he did speak he commanded the respectful attention of the Senate, and always spoke with effect. His last elaborate effort that I remember was in defense of his State, whose institutions and rights he thought had been unfairly criticised and unjustly assailed, and I question if there is on record a clearer and more convincing exposition of the rights and reserved powers of the States of the Union than is given in this speech. If he had done no other public service, this speech would entitle him to take rank among the ablest expounders of the constitutional powers of the State and Federal Governments.

It was my fortune, Mr. President, to attend the funeral ceremonies of this venerable and distinguished Senator at his home in Providence, and the large attendance from other States, the outpouring on that occasion of all classes and conditions in that community to do honor to their fellow-citizen and dead statesman, bore evidence of how much he was beloved by his neighbors and how highly he was esteemed by his fellow-countrymen. It is drawing no invidious distinction to say that no Senator has ever gone out of this Chamber to his last account more universally respected and lamented than Governor ANTHONY; few Senators ever served a constituency longer, and none more faithfully. His long and distinguished public career is closed without a shadow to dim its luster or a suspicion upon his integrity to mar its completeness.

Remarks by Mr. INGALLS, of Kansas.

The service of Senator ANTHONY in this body exceeded the entire period of Republican ascendency, from Lincoln to Garfield—a momentous interval, characterized by unprecedented activity of the material, intellectual, and moral energies of the nation, and resulting in structural changes in government and society.

It was an epoch of tremendous passions; of vague and indefinite morality; of frenzied debate; of anomalous statesmanship. There were giants in those days, and when the Macaulay of another age shall turn to rehearse their history, he will find little in our recorded annals to explain the remarkable and long-continued prominence of Senator ANTHONY in his State and the country, or the extraordinary influence he exercised upon all his contemporaries.

Without the learning and eloquence of Sumner, the logic of Fessenden, the restless industry of Wilson, or the intense and relentless energy of Chandler and Morton, he was the trusted counselor and companion of all, and was accorded the highest positions of confidence and honor to which a Senator can aspire.

For twenty-five years Senator ANTHONY uttered no word
in debate in this Chamber that is not recorded, but how
faint and unsatisfactory is the portrait that this will present
to posterity. Those who recall the melody of his diction
and the dignity of his delivery will always wonder with regret that he so seldom spoke who spoke so well; but no
printed page could record the gentle and benignant courtesy
which shone in his demeanor and lent a nameless but irre-
sistible charm to his deportment and bearing; the confident
courage that despised the paltry arts and the hollow clamors
of the demagogue; the stainless honor that knew no taint
of perfidy or guile.

He was a minister of grace. He never made an enemy and
never lost a friend. The envy that might have been aroused
by his early success was averted by the sensitive delicacy of
his nature; and the jealousy that might have been excited
by his long supremacy was disarmed by his loyalty to his
friends, by his fidelity to his convictions, by his unsullied
integrity, by the temperate restraint of his spirit which no
heat of controversy could disturb nor any rancor of partisanship provoke to retaliation unworthy of a Christian and
a gentleman.

The entire career of Senator ANTHONY was one of unique
and singular felicity. For him fate spared its irony. Nem-
esis was propitiated. Fortune favored him. Time denied
him none of those possessions that are regarded as the
chief requisites of human happiness. He escaped calumny,
and detraction passed him by. There was no winter in his
years. He had length of days without infirmity. His ambition was satisfied. Honor, health, love, friendship, affluence,
which so often with capricious disdain elude the most stren-

nous pursuit, attended him as courtiers surround a monarch. His life was not fragmentary and unfinished, but full-orbed and complete. Death was not an interruption, but a climax. His sun was neither obscured nor eclipsed, but followed its appointed path to the western horizon. So he departed, and above his spirit and his fame abides the enduring covenant of peace:

> His memory, like a cloudless sky;
> His conscience, like a sea at rest.

Remarks by Mr. HAWLEY, of Connecticut.

Mr. PRESIDENT: So much has been said by many who knew Mr. ANTHONY long and well that much speaking by me is neither needed nor becoming.

He was a most devoted, reverent, and obedient servant of his State. He was very proud of the trust Rhode Island reposed in him. He was an American, a patriot, a lover of liberty and union in every fiber of his being. Submissive to the Divine will and fearless of death, he yet wished to live, and I think he longed to complete thirty years of Senatorship. During the last few months of his life he earnestly desired to return to Washington, and could he have chosen the place of departure I believe he would have selected this Capitol.

In speaking to the memory of Henry Wilson he said:

Nor was the occasion of his death inappropriate to his life. It has been lamented that the inevitable hour found him away from his home and without the tender ministrations of woman. In this regret I do not share. * * * Where should the patriot statesman whose life has been devoted to freedom die rather than in the Capitol, whose uplifted Dome bears aloft the vindicated statue of Liberty?

In the succeeding paragraph, which the Senator from Massachusetts has already quoted, Mr. ANTHONY refers in lines of exquisite delicacy and feeling to the circumstances of domestic bereavement and loneliness in which his own domestic life was a parallel to Mr. Wilson's, and adds:

He had nothing left to love but his country. It was proper, then, that he should die here, where his greatest work has been wrought; here, where his greatest triumphs had been achieved.

Mr. ANTHONY possessed a strong, deep, loving nature, though not demonstrative or careless of choice, and he grappled his friends with hooks of steel. Senators who heard it cannot forget the fervor and profound pathos of his lamentation over the loss of his beloved and inseparable friend Burnside.

In some characteristics he gave evidence of the teachings of Quaker ancestry, molding a congenial nature. His courtesy and gentleness, his pleasing tone of voice, his love of peace, his refined wit and humor, his tender poetic sentiment, his fund of literary, historical, and political reminiscences made him most welcome in many circles of admiring and attached friends here and elsewhere.

His classical education, his reading, and his more than twenty years of successful experience as an editor, beginning at the age of twenty-three, gave him a charming and polished style as a writer, of which he has left admirable illustrations in many addresses. Of his varied services, and especially of his zealous and effective labors during the stormy years of war, my seniors in this Hall have spoken. Personally I was nearly four years associated with him in that committee of which he was twenty-one years the chairman. His society made labor agreeable. All sense of drudgery was lost in the pleasure of social intercourse.

Connecticut will join her neighbor of two hundred and fifty years of unbroken friendship in tributes of respect to the memory of the distinguished and honored citizen who has gone to " the sublime equality and sacred fraternity of the tomb."

When all things move in what we imagine to be the due course of nature, as year after year hurries along, the Divine Father greatly mitigates the dread of death. Before one reaches the allotted three-score and ten, the time comes when he feels that the majority of all whom he could know well and love well have gone over to the other side. The sound of a tree that has fallen in the forest becomes a familiar sound, no longer alarming. The multitude of old and dear friends, who are invisible but still very real, occupy more and more of our thoughts. Calling our faith and philosophy to our aid, we try to believe that it is not death we dread, but dying. We get so weary of eternal turmoil that in despondent hours we fancy that we can almost envy that brilliant soldier of the late war whose last words were, " Let us cross the river and rest in the shade."

Our friend could not have been surprised by his summons. It is a comforting belief, and let us try to indulge it, that he is fully at peace in the society of the host of his friends and colaborers who have preceded him.

Said a Greek poet:

> Little it imports
> The dead, I think, if any shall obtain
> Magnificent and costly obsequies;
> Vain affectation of the living, this.

But no one has gone from us who would feel a richer joy to know that all men speak of him kindly and lovingly.

Remarks by Mr. MANDERSON, of Nebraska.

Mr. PRESIDENT: The eloquent tributes to the noble dead whose virtues we extol to-day from those who have been his coworkers in the Senate during the eventful years when HENRY B. ANTHONY did his full duty here would seem to have so fully met the demands of reverence and affection that it was not needed that one who so lately came to full personal appreciation of his noble qualities should be heard in words of eulogy; yet I cannot resist the opportunity offered me to speak of the high esteem in which I held him during the many years when to me he was simply one of the most prominent of public men, and of how much I came to revere and love him when it became my great privilege to know him personally.

I can never forget the cordiality of the welcome extended when I became his associate in the public work to which he had brought such high appreciation and advantageous effort; the encouraging words and valuable aid given me by the noble son of Rhode Island will ever remain in my memory as one of its most valued treasures. The mere acquaintance of the latter part of the Forty-seventh Congress ripened into something stronger during the winter of 1883–'84, and when, during the last summer, it was my fortune to spend a few delightful days with him at Block Island, in the State he loved so dearly, and when I saw him surrounded by his neighbors, relatives, and friends, an admiring acquaintanceship became a warm friendship.

Coming to the United States Senate in 1859, and serving there for the next quarter of a century, Governor ANTHONY was an active participant, if not a leader, in the most important legislative affairs during those eventful years of the Republic. He took his seat at the time when partisan spirit and sectional politics were at the flood. During the dark and gloomy days of the war of rebellion he did his full duty to the country he had sworn to protect and serve. His voice was ever raised for the cause of the right. He could find no excuses for rebellion and did not attempt to palliate treason. Too gentle in nature to be fiercely denunciatory of the misguided and misled men who were engaged in that which he deemed to be an unholy and inexcusable crusade against the dearest and best interests of the Republic and a base attack upon the rights of man, yet he had none but words of condemnation for their course and of strong support and hearty help for the soldiers of the nation. Those who wore the blue ever found in him a friend.

The dreadful conflict over, his shaping hand and controlling brain may be seen in the measures of reconstruction and the important laws designed to cement a divided nation and bring again together the warring States, that they might once more dwell in unity and peace.

Twenty-five years of intelligent, active, painstaking, appreciative performance of his arduous and perplexing duties! How grand the record! There was much during the time to perplex and annoy, a great deal of a nature calculated to change the patient, loving spirit into one impatient and petulant, but no colleague in the Senate, constituent in his State, or fellow-citizen of HENRY B. ANTHONY ever found such change.

The poet of the early English, grand Geoffrey Chaucer, says, "He is a gentleman who does gentle deeds;" and the life of our departed friend is so full of the constant performance of such deeds that he made himself of the true gentry and issued his own patent to nobility. He did not seem to tire of such well-doing; the passing of the years and the coming on of old age brought physical change, but "that good gray head which all men knew" was ever the servant of the kind heart. He seemed to have followed the sound advice of the old philosopher, and to be able "to resist with success the frigidity of old age by combining the body, the mind, and the heart, keeping these in parallel vigor by exercise, study, and love."

But I do not propose any review of the noble life that has gone or to comment upon the valuable lessons that it teaches. Others have done it far more profitably than I could hope to do. In one official capacity, however, it seems fitting that I should speak of the lamented dead. At an early period in his life Mr. ANTHONY assumed editorial charge of the leading newspaper of his native State and made the Providence Journal a power for good. It was a fitting recognition of his intimate knowledge of the printer's craft that prompted the Senate in December, 1859, to place him upon the Committee on Printing. He served continuously upon this committee for nearly twenty-five years, and for twenty years of this period he was its alert, attentive, accommodating, and efficient chairman.

During the first year of Senator ANTHONY's service upon the committee, at a time when the political party with which he acted was in the minority, investigations were made of the contract system under which the printing and binding for the Government had been performed. This investigation showed so many abuses, so much of favoritism and fraud, that the result was the purchase of a printing office, of small size and insufficient in its appointments, which grew with the country's needs and growth to its present immense proportions. In the management of this office, and in its gradual enlargement as the work done there has increased, Senator ANTHONY took a deep interest.

The busy hive, with its thousands of industrious, intelligent employés, whose active brains and deft fingers furnish to the world the best public literature it has ever read; with its mighty forces, steam and electricity, giving life and motion to delicate machinery that seems to think and reason as it performs its allotted task—this great Printing Office, throbbing and pulsating day and night for the public good, stands as a mighty monument to the dead ANTHONY.

The record of the proceedings in the Senate bear testimony to his repeated efforts (unfortunately not often crowned with success) to diminish the cost of the public printing by curtailing the amount and dispensing with masses of official verbiage which now swell too many of the public documents. He had a true man's hatred of "shams," and made bold assaults upon many of the works of deceit where they lay strongly intrenched.

One of the abuses which he sought persistently to do away with was the cumbering of the Congressional Record with remarks alleged to have been made, but never delivered, in Congress. Permit me to give an extract from one of the latest speeches made by him, and which, listened to with great interest in the Senate, should have brought forth abundant legislative fruit:

Whatever may be said of the unimportant character of too much of the debates of Congress, as of other deliberative bodies, the importance of the proceedings can hardly be overestimated, and upon these the debates throw great light. They are the proceedings which establish and modify the Government of forty millions of free, active, adventurous people, and whatever makes these proceedings plainer is of high value to the people, by whose servants they are transacted.

Further on he said:

The Congressional Record should be what it purports to be. Its phonographic accuracy and completeness should mirror exactly what is said and done. It should speak, like a credible witness, "the truth, the whole truth, and nothing but the truth." Its correctness is the essential quality of its value. If not correct it is not only useless but injurious; it deceives instead of informing, it misleads instead of guiding, and throws confusion upon what it undertakes to enlighten.

Words of wisdom these, and abundantly worthy of the man who uttered them.

Another matter is well worthy of note as showing the sense of fairness that characterized the late chairman of the Committee on Printing. In the early days of his service investigation showed that many scandalous frauds had attended the purchase of paper and other material used in the public printing. These were done away with by changes in the law conceived and carried into execution by Governor ANTHONY. Purchases made in open market from favorites were no longer countenanced. Advertisements are now made for sealed proposals to supply according to samples furnished to each bidder, and bids are opened in public by the Joint Committee on Printing, and awards made to the lowest bidder who will best subserve the interests of the Government.

But I need not deal in further detail. Our brother's life was open as the day; he knew not concealments. So many were his virtues that "none knew him but to love him."

A life of virtue and well-doing prepared him for the great end. As his life had been so was his death. It was most fitting that it should come to him quietly, gently, and without shock.

He was to all of us most excellent example, and like him

So may'st thou live till like ripe fruit thou drop
Into thy mother's lap, or be with ease
Gathered, not harshly plucked, for death mature.

Remarks by Mr. SHEFFIELD, of Rhode Island.

Mr. PRESIDENT: As I recall the intimate personal relations which existed between the late Senator ANTHONY and myself for a period of forty years and upwards, the pleasure I have felt from his society, the wisdom I have derived from his counsel, the many acts of kindness I have received at his hands, and my attachment to his person, I hardly dare to trust myself to review his life and character in the presence of so many reminders of his death. This Chamber was the scene of his long-continued and useful service to his country. The presence of his honored associates to pay a tribute to his exalted worth, and my own entry here to occupy the place his death made vacant, bring before my mind in bold outline the genial man whom I could have wished would have lived always.

No Senator long acquainted with Mr. ANTHONY will arise to address the Senate on this occasion without having in mind the eulogies pronounced upon deceased Senators by him, eulogies which welled up from a mind and heart filled with human sympathy, as pure water from a natural spring, and expressed in language as pure as the fountain in which those eulogies originated; and especially will each Senator recall the burning words with which Mr. ANTHONY, as the representative of the Senate, delivered to the authorities of Massachusetts under the dome of its capitol the dead body of a great Senator; but the voice then so eloquent over the remains of Sumner is now hushed in death. The brilliant imagination which then mingled sadness and triumph has now been put out forever.

Well may we say:

> Who would not sing for Lycidas? He knew
> Himself to sing, and build the lofty rhyme;
> He must not float upon his watery bier
> Unwept, and welter to the parching wind
> Without the meed of some melodious tear.

Mr. ANTHONY was a lineal descendant of John Anthony, a native of Hempstead in England, who came to Boston in the Hercules in 1634, and to Rhode Island soon after 1640. Gilbert Stuart, the artist, whose mother was an Anthony, who has preserved on canvas so faithfully the features of Washington, descended from the same ancestor. William Anthony was the father of Senator ANTHONY, and his mother was a daughter of James Greene, of Warwick. The Warwick Greenes have been a conspicuous family in Rhode Island from the foundation of the Colony. General Nathanael Greene, whose statue adorns a place in a hall of this Capitol, and Col. Ray Greene, who commanded at the battle of Red Bank, were members of this family, and two of its representatives have been members of the Senate. The ancestors of Governor ANTHONY belonged to the Society of Friends, which for a considerable time in our colonial history was the most influential denomination of Christians in the Colony. After Mr. ANTHONY graduated from college, he went to reside for a time and engaged in some mercantile pursuit at Savannah. He returned to Rhode Island, and was there married to Sarah Aborn, daughter of the late Christopher Rhodes, in 1837. In 1838, at the age of twenty-three, he assumed the editorial control of the Providence Journal.

At that time, and for more than a score of years thereafter, he was surrounded by a coterie of young men, mostly college

5 A

friends, of learning, wit, and of marked ability as writers, who aided him more or less in the conduct of his paper. But while his associates contributed to its success, his was the critical judgment, the controlling mind, which carried the Journal to the front rank of the New England press, a standing which it yet maintains. In the heated contests which preceded the insurrection in the State in 1842, and during and subsequent to that event, while a constitution for the State was being framed and adopted, the Journal was the organ of the Government, and the distinguished ability with which it was conducted brought Mr. ANTHONY prominently before the people of the State, and in 1849 he was presented by the young Whigs as their candidate for governor, an office to which he was elected that year, and re-elected in 1850, when he declined to be further a candidate for the office. In 1854 the great sorrow which ever after shadowed somewhat the life of Governor ANTHONY fell upon him. On the 12th of July of that year his wife died. I might pause here to dwell upon the tenderness of his nature as developed by that affliction, but the theme is too sacred—I will not sully it. Burdened with this great sorrow, early in 1855 he visited Europe for rest and relief. Upon his return he resumed control of his paper.

Governor ANTHONY inherited from his father an interest in a manufacturing establishment located in his native town of Coventry. Though for a time he was interested in carrying on business at this establishment, he retired from it when he went abroad, but omitted to give notice of his withdrawal. In 1857 the company became involved in the financial distress of that time. The creditors claimed that Governor ANTHONY was liable for the debts of the company. He did not stop to have the question of his liability for these debts settled in the courts, but manfully came forward and met them, and honorably settled the claims made upon him. This added to his popularity, and in 1859, after a sharp contest, he was elected to the Senate of the United States, and to this office he was four times re-elected. This shows alike the stability of the character of the Senator and of the people of the State who elected him. While in the Senate during this most interesting period of our national history the conduct of Senator ANTHONY was seen and known of all men.

As an editor, Mr. ANTHONY clearly comprehended the rights and duties of his office. He understood the wants and necessities of the industrial interests of New England, of which Providence is a great center, and it was his laudable ambition to make his paper a leading advocate and organ of those interests. He thought clearly and selected with rapidity the words which could best express his thoughts in the most forcible manner. There was no room left for construction in what he wrote. His style was direct, clear, and forcible, without excess of verbiage—it needed no interpreter. When he entered the Senate he had no superior in New England in writing effective editorial paragraphs, and though his Senatorial career was correct and very creditable to himself, it may be well doubted if he had continued in his profession whether his fame as an editor would not have been as desirable as it is as a Senator.

As a politician Mr. ANTHONY stood by his party, seeking to correct its errors and to improve its policy within and not without its lines. He always adhered with fidelity to his convictions of duty, yet he always treated his opponents with a generous justice, while that treatment was duly appreciated, and when it was not he was yet just. He won the respect and regard of the opposing party by tempering the expression of his convictions with evidences of good nature and with an address which conciliated rather than repelled them.

The secret of Mr. ANTHONY'S influence was an entire frankness, the natural outcome of his character, with his absolute integrity of purpose, which prevented him from supporting any measure which he believed to be prejudicial to the best interests of the public. In the Senate he never made the most of himself, for he always underrated his own capabilities in comparison with the capabilities of others. He was careful never to undertake what he feared he might not be able to accomplish.

Mr. ANTHONY was a man of amiable and even of fascinating manners, deferential to those about him, and mindful of all the proprieties of life; he was well calculated to impress with a sense of regard and respect all with whom he was brought into close relations; never obtrusive, full of conversational resources, endowed with a ready wit and a rich fund of pleasing anecdotes always at command to illustrate a point without encumbering it; strong in his friendships, tender in his sensibilities, yet with absolute self-control. That he was a student of the science of government apart from his observation of the practice of that science in the Senate, no one will pretend; and while he could state a point which would expose a defect in the argument of an adversary as clearly and as effectively as any of his compeers, he was not the man to present by public address a subject involving complicated details. He rather directed his force against an adversary by isolated assaults at his weak points than by an attack upon his entire line—by sortie, rather than by siege. He was a conciliatory man, and was possessed of great forbearance. He would go to the very verge of propriety to avoid the giving of offense, and would exhaust the resources of a very charitable disposition before he would believe that cause for offense was intended to be given to him.   But there was a line which his self-respect would not allow him to pass or an adversary to cross, and when forced to resistance he was a vigorous and unyielding adversary.

Mr. ANTHONY loved his native State.   He was devoted to its institutions and thoroughly imbued with the spirit of its history.   He believed with Lord Coleridge that the character of a state was not to be determined by the number of acres of ground it contained or by the number of its population, but rather by the characters and achievements of its people.   In quiet retirement, in company with men of kindred thoughts, in conversation Mr. ANTHONY dwelt with admiration upon the fortitude and self-denial of those exiles of exiles who settled the Rhode Island Colony; upon their sufferings and hardships, and withal upon the Christian charity which they exhibited in planting and maintaining the great ideas upon which the Colony was founded.   Then he would trace the progress of the colonial history, the growth of the Colony, and its development into a State; the rise of its commerce until its canvas whitened every sea; and that commerce alone, and the commercial enterprise of its people, merited the glowing eulogy of Burke in the House of Commons upon the commercial enterprise of all the Colonies.   Then he would describe how wars and the adverse policy of the Government drove that commerce from the ocean, and forced upon reluctant New England a blessing in disguise, that wiser policy, which the great commoner of Kentucky called "the American system" of fostering and protecting American industries; and how Rhode Island, upon the ruins of its commercial industries, reared factories and workshops and operated them, until their handiwork under the operation of this benign system won for them a place among the foremost industries of the country. At these times he would also delight to dwell upon the men who had illustrated Rhode Island history and their achievements, to show the claims of Rhode Island upon the National Union, a part of which achievements he appeared to feel to be his by inheritance from a line of ancestors who had borne an important part in settling, developing, and maintaining the Colony and State during every period of its history.

The grave has closed over him and shut in his mortal remains. Throughout his life he anticipated the harvest of a good name, and he did nothing to blight it. His end did not come until after a long career of useful public service, when his physical energies had been exhausted and the ends of life had been attained. It is a sad thought; but it will not be long before "our lighted torches will pass to other hands."

Senator ANTHONY was a fortunate man; fortunate in his moral and intellectual endowments; fortunate in his friends and in his surroundings; fortunate in his life, fortunate in his death in his own house with kind friends around him. He has left no stain upon his good name; his finished course covers nothing to be regretted, leaves undone nothing desired, but that his career could have been prolonged and that his usefulness could have been continued. But it has been otherwise ordered, and his friends should be thankful for the blessings which his life has conferred, rather than to murmur at the Providence which has determined it.

Mr. President, I second the resolutions on your table.

The PRESIDENT *pro tempore.* The question is on agreeing to the resolutions.

The resolutions were agreed to unanimously; and (at two o'clock and fifty minutes p. m.) the Senate adjourned.

PROCEEDINGS IN THE HOUSE OF REPRESENTATIVES.

WEDNESDAY, JANUARY 21, 1885.

At the appointed hour of four o'clock, Mr. Speaker Carlisle, in accordance with previous action, laid before the House the resolutions of the Senate in relation to the death of the late Senator ANTHONY; which were read by the Clerk, as follows:

IN THE SENATE OF THE UNITED STATES,

January 19, 1885.

Resolved, That the Senate has heard with profound sorrow of the death of HENRY B. ANTHONY, late a Senator from the State of Rhode Island.

Resolved, That the business of the Senate be now suspended, to enable his associates to pay proper tribute of regard to his high character and distinguished public services.

Resolved, That the Secretary of the Senate communicate these resolutions to the House of Representatives.

Resolved, That, as an additional mark of respect to the memory of the deceased, the Senate do now adjourn.

Mr. CHACE, of Rhode Island. I offer the following resolutions, which I ask the Clerk to read.

The Clerk read as follows:

Resolved, That the House of Representatives has received with deep sorrow the official announcement of the death of HENRY BOWEN ANTHONY, late United States Senator from the State of Rhode Island.

Resolved, That the business of the House be now suspended, that opportunity may be afforded to give expression of our sense of his personal worth, of his public services, and of the loss which the country and his native State have sustained.

Resolved, That at the conclusion of these tributes to his memory the House shall stand adjourned.

71

Remarks by Mr. CHACE, of Rhode Island.

Again Rhode Island is called to mourn the loss of a distinguished son. A second time in my brief career in this House it becomes my duty to pay the last tribute of respect to the memory of one of her Senators. Again we are reminded how swiftly glide these lives of ours; that the dreams of hope are but shadows; that the honors for which we clutch must wither in our hand; that the cares, the joys, the fears of life alike soon find an end. It is well for us to pause for a brief season and look back.

When, in the closing days of 1859, the Senate of the Thirty-sixth Congress met, the two sides of that Chamber more nearly resembled the representatives of two hostile countries than an ordinary legislative body, met to calmly discuss questions of common interest. All of those wonderful intellectual giants, the product of the primitive days of the Republic, had passed off the stage of action. Clay, full of years, but weary and worn with compromise, had sunk to rest with only anxious hope, and was reposing at his own beautiful Ashland; the ashes of Calhoun were mingling with the soil of his native Carolina; Webster, almost heartbroken and full of forebodings for the future of the Union, had been laid in the simple tomb at Marshfield, where the ocean which he loved so well might sing his solemn dirge through the coming ages. The gathering storm which these men had vainly sought to avert was darkly impending over the nation. All the great economic questions were swallowed up in this one absorbing topic.

Among those who entered that Senate and took sides with the defenders of freedom was HENRY B. ANTHONY, of Rhode

Island. In the prime of life, at forty-five years of age, inheriting from a long line of virtuous ancestry a constitution of wonderful strength and vigor; of singular beauty, both of person and feature, with a commanding presence, highly educated, cultivated in his manners, with a rare grace and urbanity, and a charming felicity in social intercourse, he at once became a favorite, even in those days of intense partisanship, with members of both sides of the Senate. Possessed of intellectual gifts of the very highest order, thoroughly furnished as he was by the peculiar training which a long career of journalism had given him, he was fitted to take a high position in the councils of the nation.

Possessed of a peculiarly well-balanced mind, his caution and prudence often restrained him from labored efforts of oratory and from participating in the excitements of clashing debate. In all the legislative history of the country but few men have introduced measures of great and far-reaching importance. The qualities that dazzle and captivate the popular mind are not always those which are of most value. As in nature so in the operation of parliamentary bodies, we find the silent forces are often the most potent. It is by patient toil and careful prevision in committee that the public interests are guarded and promoted. This was the peculiar field of usefulness to which our lamented friend bent his attention. On the floor of the Senate he was alert, attentive, and careful, and when occasion required, quick to penetrate the armor of error, to expose its purpose, or to defend those measures for which the public weal called.

He did not speak often, but when his voice was heard it commanded attention. His speeches, always bearing evidence of great learning and research, were couched in the purest and most polished English.   His intellect was broad and vigorous, with wit as keen and incisive as a Damascus blade, that would have been a dangerous weapon with one less gentle, for he was as kind and loving as a woman.

In all the long list of names borne on the Senate roll two men only have been elected to five consecutive terms—Thomas H. Benton and HENRY B. ANTHONY.   And yet, although serving so long, much of the time during the most stormy period of our parliamentary history, no man of all that throng of fellow-Senators could say that he had just cause of offense toward him, and with rare exceptions all were his friends.

Serving at a time when from the necessities of the Government growing out of the war money was poured out like water, when in the mad fever of speculation and grasping for sudden wealth through Government contracts reputations went down like soldiers in battle, he came out unscathed, not a breath of suspicion resting upon him.   Holding the most pronounced views on all the questions which agitated the public mind like a seething caldron during the period before and after the war, though abating nothing, he retained the friendship of his most earnest opponents.   Knowing the weakness of indecision, he reached forward for political truth with a firm hand and still preserved a strong balance of conservatism.

Deeply learned in the foundation principles of our Government, and as deeply skilled in the use of language, he sometimes presented those principles with wonderful effect.

He was twice elected governor of Rhode Island and twice President of the United States Senate.   But long and honorable and useful as have been his services in the Senate, it is as a faithful son of Rhode Island that the citizens of that State will most cherish his memory.   Born in the town of Coventry of a Quaker family whose ancestors had dwelt there from the days of its earliest settlement, spending his youth among the hills of his native State, educated in her schools and at her university, putting forth the first labors of his early manhood as well as the more brilliant efforts of his maturer years in defense of her constitution, he loved her as a man loves his mother.

He was, indeed, a part of Rhode Island. He believed her constitution to be the most perfect instrument of the kind ever drawn by the hand of man, and his defense of it is unanswerable. His name and his fame are linked with Rhode Island and her happily constituted system. There, as a journalist, he attained a most distinguished position, building up, from small beginnings, one of the most influential and useful journals in New England; earning, by the purity of his diction, clearness and conciseness of style, and felicity of expression, a high reputation. Honored and trusted by her people, he honored them by the faithfulness of his services.

I have known Senator ANTHONY from my youth up—known him as did all, to respect, to admire, to love him. In every sphere, in all circles, under all circumstances, wherever he went, his progress was a constant conquest of friendship, and friends once won, he "grappled them to his soul with hooks of steel."

How many who commenced the race of life with him have fallen by the way while he passed on. The friends of his youth died and he found others.

During his service in the Senate he saw the shackles stricken from four million slaves, the deed of manumission written in the blood of three hundred thousand men; the Union, tottering to its foundation, purified and restored; the dream of the

fathers that this land should be consecrated to liberty realized.
During his term he saw men rise to distinction in both Houses
of Congress and pronounced their eulogies. As Senator, he
saw Lincoln inaugurated; held up his hands during the vigils
of those weary four years of war, and saw him buried, mourned
alike by friend and foe; saw Garfield rise from obscurity to
distinction in the forum, the field, and in this House—elected
Senator, made President, and laid in his grave on the shores
of Lake Erie. Grant's wonderful career from the store in
Galena to his triumphant progress around the world was but
an episode.

Of his hope for the future life I cannot speak. He rarely
spoke of it to me.

As life is ordinarily viewed, it may be said that his was a
success; but if we could go with him through the long journey, full rounded up to near three-score and ten, we might
not maintain our estimate of what is human success. He had
hosts of friends and few enemies; was honored as but few men
have been; but with all he carried for many years a great sorrow. The wife of his youth, beautiful and accomplished, was
early stricken down, and ever after he continued alone the
journey of life. He realized, as all must, that—

> All pomp was but a name;
> That gold and silver were not life and joy;
> That what to-day bestowed of love or fame,
> To-morrow's breath would wither and destroy.

He realized, as do all who grapple with great public questions, of how much too little avail are our best endeavors to
establish justice, to put an end to inequality, or to satisfy those
less favored. He saw how empty a thing is honor, what a
dream is life itself, and how decay and death follow quickly

after youth and strength, as cloud-shadows chase the sunshine on the mountain-side. Occupying as he did for many years so distinguished a position, he realized that—

> He who ascends the mountain tops shall find
> Its loftiest peaks most wrapped in clouds and snow;
> He who surpasses or subdues mankind
> Must look down on the hate of those below;
> Though far above the sun of glory glow,
> And far beneath the earth and ocean spread,
> Round him are icy rocks, and loudly blow
> Contending tempests on his naked head,
> And thus reward the toils which to those summits led.

With him "life's vain parade is over." But though "he walked with throngs of good friends, now at last he is called to pass alone the dread portals of death."

He will long be remembered by his associates here for the radiance of his genial presence, for his careful attention to every detail of legislative duty, for the warmth of his friendship, and the absence of partisan rancor. In his native State his memory will be cherished by young and old for his gentleness, his dignity, his faithfulness to trust; for his long and useful services.

Remarks by Mr. KELLEY, of Pennsylvania.

Mr. SPEAKER: I address the House not because I believe I can add anything of value to what others will say of the character and labors of the late Senator ANTHONY, but because the sweet memories of an unclouded friendship which extended through a quarter of a century and endured the friction of personal, political, and official relations impel me to offer a tribute, however unworthy of its subject it may prove to be.

HENRY B. ANTHONY entered upon the duties of Senator from the State of Rhode Island in December, 1859, at the opening of the Thirty-sixth Congress, and I entered fully upon my duties as Representative from the fourth district of Pennsylvania on the 4th of July, 1861, when the two Houses, in obedience to the proclamation of President Lincoln, met "to consider and determine such measures as in their wisdom the public safety and interest may seem to demand."

The times were disjointed before the elections of 1860 were held. The controlling spirits of the South having determined to submit the interpretation of the Constitution to the arbitrament of war, the Senators from that section of the country withdrew from the Senate, and those who had been looked to to represent the people in the House of Representatives declined to accept Congressional nominations and refused to recognize the Thirty-seventh Congress as a body whose enactments would be binding on them in law or conscience. The situation produced by this action was novel and portentous. In matters of gravest import and responsibility the Executive must act without the aid of precedent or tradition, and the President and his Cabinet naturally sought counsel from the recently chosen representatives of the loyal people. It thus came to pass that gentlemen elected to the Thirty-seventh Congress, who, under ordinary circumstances, would probably not have met until the month of December, became *habitués* of the capital and co-workers from the 4th of March, between which date and the organization of Congress I frequently met Senator ANTHONY in such social intercourse as the already disturbed condition of Washington would permit, and in consultation with the President, heads of Departments, Senators, and members-elect of the House of Representatives.

Though a man of broad and varied information and profound convictions he preferred no claim to leadership, and superficial observers more readily regarded him as a devotee to society than as an earnest man of affairs. He was in the vigor of mature manhood, and I recall with pleasure the sweet smile that wreathed his handsome face upon the slightest provocative to mirth. Within an irreverent but limited circle of acquaintances he was called "the rosebud Senator," which sobriquet might have been bestowed as a tribute to the healthful glow which mantled his cheek or from the fact that in those days when *boutonnières* were in less common use than now he constantly wore a bud or other choice flower.

He had none of the impetuosity or burning enthusiasm of Senators Wade, of Ohio, and Chandler, of Michigan, or of the intense devotion to the advanced opinions, approved by his judgment, which characterized my great colleague Thaddeus Stevens; yet he was the trusted counselor of his more impulsive fellow-Senators, and his fidelity to the convictions which sustained the Republican party and impelled its advance from point to point in the cause of personal freedom until American slavery had perished was never doubted by that imperious and exacting party leader, the great commoner of Pennsylvania.

The means of communication between the capital and remote sections of the Republic were, in comparison with those of to-day, very restricted, and the President could not with propriety name an earlier day than the 4th of July for the assembling of Congress. But that the armed forces of the improvised confederacy should be prevented from invading the capital or any of the loyal States, he had upon his own authority put seventy-five thousand men into the field to which the United States had been challenged.   When, on the designated day, Congress had assembled, the President in his message expressed the estimate of the executive department of the Government as to the draft the rebellion would make upon the resources of the Republic.   In suggesting the number of men and the amount of means he hoped Congress would provide he said, "It is now recommended that you give the legal means for making this contest a short and decisive one; that you place at the control of the Government for the work at least four hundred thousand men and four hundred million dollars."

From that day until Grant had restored to Lee his sword, the surrender of which had symbolized the defeat of the confederate army and the collapse of the pretended government which had called it into existence, until the work of reconstruction had been completed, so far as legislation could promote its completion, the opinions of Senator ANTHONY were sought and weighed by the Executive and those legislators who from their greater prominence in the proceedings of Congress were popularly regarded as the men who were shaping the destinies of our country.   His judgment was rarely or never at fault.   He seemed to comprehend every question as it arose, whether it was a measure to provide men and means for successful warfare; or to establish a system of finance which should, without embarrassing the productive interests of the country, enable the Government to furnish the Army and Navy with the amplest munitions of war; or to restore to the position in the Union they had sought to abandon the impoverished and decimated States of the South; or to reduce our revenues without impairing the public credit by the repeal of many of the taxes which had been adopted as a war measure, and which bore, as all internal or excise taxes must bear, specially upon the producing classes.

Caution is the parent of prudence, and caution was a marked characteristic of Senator ANTHONY. While appreciating the greatness of the duties before the Government, he would delay, if not postpone indefinitely, the adoption as a policy of any measure or set of measures that seemed to involve the possibility of encouraging the enemies of the Government by the abandonment of a declared purpose. It was this characteristic which, above all others, secured him the supreme confidence of President Lincoln, whose caution is now seen to have been as efficient in bringing the war to a successful close as were the skill and courage of the most brilliant of our soldiers.

But I am trespassing upon the time of the House, my object in addressing which was, as I have said, to simply lay a humble tribute on the bier of a long-cherished friend.

Remarks by Mr. POLAND, of Vermont.

Mr. SPEAKER: I should hardly have felt justified in occupying a moment on this occasion except for the fact that I am one of the few members of this House who served in the other with the deceased Senator ANTHONY.

My acquaintance with him commenced with the opening of the Thirty-ninth Congress, the first Congress after the close of the great war. The ten years which followed were as trying and difficult to the men engaged in the administration of public affairs as any in our history. The questions as to how the seceding States were to be restored to their proper places in the Union, how peace and harmony were to be again restored, and the whole country again united after the fearful

6 A

disruption, and the financial question of how to provide for the immense indebtedness, were all new and difficult, and might well appall and distract the wisest statesman. The proper settlement of some of these questions was embarrassed and complicated by the bitterness and acrimony naturally engendered by the losses and sufferings caused by the war.

Having been in Congress myself during the ten years succeeding the war, I feel justified in saying that Senator ANTHONY bore a much more important part and exercised a much greater influence in the proper settlement of all these great questions than he was generally credited with in the country. He made no pretension to oratory, and did not mingle largely in general debate. But his associates soon learned his value, the breadth and solidity of his judgment, his extended and accurate knowledge upon all public questions, and he exercised the influence accorded to a wise and sagacious man. While the war was waging he gave most earnest and vigorous effort to make it successful. When it was over, he ranked among those who desired in settling and adjusting the questions growing out of it to show all possible kindness and magnanimity.

The Senator was exceedingly ready and adroit in practical suggestions to meet and avoid difficulties which arose in the routine of legislative business.

I may be pardoned for relating an instance when he relieved me from a great embarrassment. Members who were here from 1865 to 1875 will remember that during that period the great work of revising the national statutes was begun and completed. I was chairman of the committee on the revision in the House and had the general charge of the matter before Congress. The revision as reported by the commissioners to

Congress was printed on large paper, in coarse type, like ordinary bills, making a very large bulk. The amendments proposed by the committee and adopted by the House numbered many hundreds.'

The rules of the House required the whole bill and all the amendments to be engrossed on paper by the Clerk before being sent to the Senate. As this would consume a great deal of time, the House, upon my application, suspended this rule, and allowed the bill to be engrossed by incorporating the amendments into one of the printed copies of the bill, by interlining, writing on the margin, or pasting on such amendments as were too long to be written in. In this form the revision was sent to and passed by the Senate. The joint rule of the two Houses requires that a bill passed by both Houses shall be engrossed on parchment to be sent to the President. This would require a great amount of time, and the end of the session was approaching. The House thereupon passed a joint resolution to suspend the joint rule for the engrossment on parchment, and authorized another copy to be prepared as before to be sent to the President. This joint resolution came back from the Senate disagreed to. Senator Garrett Davis, of Kentucky, a most excellent gentleman, but who tolerated no innovation upon established usages and ancient ways, led the opposition, and was horrified at the notion of sending such a patched bundle to the President to be preserved in the solemn archives of the State Department. The House asked a conference. I was one on the part of the House, Senator Davis one from the Senate, and he stood for a parchment engrossment of the whole Revised Statutes. I was in a great dilemma. I had given years of work to it and had obtained its passage through Congress, but it was likely to fail because I could not get it to the President for his signature. Fortunately Senator ANTHONY was one of the Senate conferees, and he proposed that the whole be reprinted and send it to the President in that form. I supposed that would take too long, but the Congressional Printer was sent for, who said it could be done in a week, and thereupon Senator ANTHONY's proposition was reported by the conference and adopted. I think I ought to finish this story by saying that the whole work was set up and printed at the Government Printing Office in three days and brought to me on the morning of the fourth day in a handsomely bound volume, which I still keep as the earliest edition of that work.

He was utterly without ostentation. He disliked all show and parade. His manners and habits were of the plainest and simplest character. One of the pleasantest recollections of my life is of a somewhat protracted visit I made him in his plain, quiet, quaint old home in the city of Providence. He was a thorough scholar and a clear and forcible writer. His long connection with the public press, his ability as a writer, and the fairness and candor with which he discussed public questions enabled him to do much in shaping the public judgment of the country during the eventful years of his manhood.

But the crowning glory of our deceased friend was the perfect kindness and amiability of his character. His heart warmed to all men. Perhaps he had enemies, but I never heard of one. His culture and his character seemed to combine in some of his literary composition. On some occasions of this kind, when called upon to pay tribute to the memory of a deceased friend or colleague, his efforts have equaled in tenderness of thought and beauty of expression anything I have ever heard or read. I have known no man whose whole life was more charming. All his words and deeds, both public and private, seemed imbued with the spirit of the holy evangel, "On earth peace, good will toward men."

Remarks by Mr. MORSE, of Massachusetts.

MR. SPEAKER: It may be presumptuous on my part to rise on the floor of this House to attempt to deliver a eulogy on the late Senator ANTHONY, but being beloved by the people of my State as much as he was in his own, and particularly so by the people of my district, I feel it my duty in their behalf to say a few words.

Mr. Speaker, so closely allied are the neighboring States of Rhode Island and Massachusetts in martial renown, in commercial interests, and in social ties, that I feel it to be my duty, as it is my pleasure, to cast my humble tribute on the grave of HENRY BOWEN ANTHONY. We knew him well in Massachusetts as the editor of the Providence Journal, which has a large circulation in the southeastern portion of our State; we respected him as the governor of our sister State, proud of her history and a stalwart defender of her institutions; we honored him as a Senator who represented the smallest of States, but whose noble intellect and patriotic heart covered the length and breadth of our great Union; and we loved him as an honorable gentleman, without fear and without reproach, who has during the last quarter of a century played important political and social parts in the great drama of life performed on this busy Washington stage.

Others have eloquently narrated the successive events of his life. My own personal acquaintance with him in this Capitol was mainly concerning those matters which had been referred to the Naval Committees of the Senate and the House, of which we were respectively members. He having served on the Naval Committee of the Senate from 1863 until his death continuously (and having again and again declined its chairmanship because he preferred to remain chairman of the Committee on Printing), he was well acquainted with the condition and the needs of our gallant Navy, its officers, its navy-yards, its academy and school. Officers of merit, with untarnished records, found in him a friend and an advocate. He was, however, sternly opposed to the retention on the quarter-deck of those whose known indulgency rendered them at times unfit to command without jeopardizing the safety of the vessels and the men under their command.

Intercourse with Senator ANTHONY on public and private business was at all times attractive and acceptable. Few members of Congress have retained during twenty-five years of continuous service, amid the labors, the intrigues, and the conflicts of political life, so many of the sterling, manly qualities which are here destroyed.

His character as a statesman, as a citizen, and as a friend was so truly and so lovingly portrayed at his funeral by Rev. Augustus Woodbury, his religious adviser and the chaplain of his deceased associate, General Burnside, that I annex the funeral discourse to these remarks.*

When Senator ANTHONY was here last winter the stamp of illness was on his features, but he had the same ease and grace of manner and conversation which had so endeared him to his friends when he was in health, and he spoke of his bodily

* The eloquent funeral discourse by the Rev. Augustus Woodbury, which was read in the House of Representatives by direction of Mr. Morse, will be found on pages 5-15.

troubles with calm composure. Before the summer months had ended he had gone to his rest, surrounded by his relatives and friends, with the beauty of the setting sun, after having lived out what the psalmist calls "the days of our age," adorned with the richest virtues of the heart. He has gone, full of years and honors, to meet the experiences of another world. Nothing is left but sweet remembrances of his purity of character, his generosity and liberality of spirit, his proud and noble manhood.

> Immortality o'ersweeps
> All pains, all tears, all time, all fears, and peals
> Like the eternal thunders of the deep
> Into our ears this truth, He lives forever.

Remarks by Mr. KEIFER, of Ohio.

Mr. SPEAKER: Again the Congress of the United States pauses in its important legislative duties to commemorate the illustrious dead.

HENRY BOWEN ANTHONY, of Rhode Island, though much my senior, was my personal friend.

He was born April 1, 1815, in the State he served so long and so well. He graduated at Brown University in 1833. He was five times elected by his State to full.terms in the United States Senate. He was an honored member of that august legislative body from March 4, 1859, to September 2, 1884, the date of his death.

At twenty-three years of age he entered upon the highly honorable work of a journalist in his native State. He never entirely gave up the profession of journalism. In 1850 and 1851 he was governor of his State, and served it acceptably.

He was then a Whig. He was a born gentleman, of Anglo-Saxon blood and Quaker principles. His generous, kind, and genial nature seemed to save him from many of the hard blows that most great men have to receive in a successful life. He was just and considerate to friend and foe, never arrogant. He was charitable and never ostentatious. He did not rely on high public position to attain name or fame, but upon accomplished deeds. He was a patient toiler after useful knowledge, and when acquired he wielded it for his country's good. A single fact with him was prized more highly than a volume of loose generalization. He had a critical constituency to watch him in his public life. It was exacting, but not unreasonable. Another has well said:

He was a stalwart champion of Rhode Island, of her sons and daughters, of her traditions and her institutions.

He personified in his whole life, as citizen, editor, chief executive of his State, Senator, and presiding officer of the United States Senate, the true type of an American gentleman. He has been aptly called the "gentleman-statesman." He lacked none of the noble qualities of a high-spirited American. He was ever keenly sensible to all the manly qualities. He was filled with convictions, and they were his own. His views are impressed upon many of the laws of his country.

His Senatorial life began when rebellion and treason were ripening in and around this Capitol. He saw both rise in the full bloom of defiant power, and then fall prostrate by the judgment of war. He never faltered in his patriotism, and when war came he held up the hands of President Lincoln from Bull Run to Appomattox. His was not a blind patriotism, but an enlightened devotion to a country he loved.

He hated slavery because he believed it was an obstacle in the progressive march of civilization and condemned by Christianity. He spoke and voted for every measure looking to the eradication of the institution of slavery in the United States and of every other injustice incident to that institution. He favored all the amendments to the Constitution of the United States adopted since the war. He was for universal amnesty and universal suffrage.

He was twice elected (March, 1863, and March, 1871) President *pro tempore* of the Senate, and in that position served four years. He displayed rare abilities as a parliamentarian and presiding officer. His principal committee work was on the Naval and Public Printing Committees. He was chairman of the latter committee for twenty-one years. He served with distinction on other standing and special committees during and since the war.

During his chairmanship of the Committee on Public Printing and under his direction great improvements were made in the character and speedy execution of the public printing. Under his master care and wise counsel the most wonderful and extensive printing establishment in the world has grown up.

He was not a frequent debater on the floor of the Senate, though the Congressional Globe and Record contain many of his eloquent speeches on important subjects. He talked when he had something useful to say. He always, when speaking, commanded the attention of the Senate. His nearest and most confidential friend, Maj. Ben: Perley Poore, speaking of his addresses, says:

His eloquence is practical and sensible, unadorned with worthless verbal embroidery, yet throughout its solid Senatorial sentences there is a classic grace .that charms the ear, while his dignified presence, pleasing manner, and pleasant voice aid in gratifying the audience.

He was bold and honest in the expression of his views, and thus made himself felt in public affairs. He loved the editorial profession, and always tried to ennoble it and give it greater weight and more universal influence for good.

Speaking in the Senate on this subject, he said:

I know something about the management of a newspaper. It is almost the only matter that I do know anything about; and for the truth of the maxim which I am about to declare I appeal to those Senators, on both sides of the Chamber, who, if they have not had greater experience than I have in that honorable profession, have reflected greater credit upon it. It is this: A paper that cannot support itself cannot be of any service to a party; to depend upon it is like leaning upon a man who cannot stand up; to spend money upon it is like wasting fuel in the attempt to kindle a stone. The day when such papers were read has passed; and the day has long since arrived when a paper, to be of service to a party, must first establish a value to the public. It must acquire a character for the reliability of its facts and for the candor of its arguments; it must have the public confidence before it can affect the public opinion; it must be in a considerable degree independent of party before a party can derive any great value from its services. Of all the foolish expenditures that are made for political purposes, none are more useless and wasteful than those for the support of the class of newspapers that very few read and that nobody believes.

Senator ANTHONY'S services to his country in time of war had substantial recognition by the District of Columbia Commandery of the Military Order of the Loyal Legion. He was the first man elected by it a companion of the third class, a degree conferred only on civilians who rendered distinguished service to their country in the war of the rebellion. The resolutions adopted by that commandery after his death are considered worthy of repetition here.

Mr. ANTHONY, by his kind consideration for others, was in all social circles a special favorite. In private conversation he had the rare quality of being a respectful listener, while at the same time he was an entertaining talker.

Though advanced in years, and decorated with well-earned public honors, he never spoke of himself or his acts with pride or egotism. Retrospection is a habit of the mind in the aged, and there is no reason why they should not speak with pride of their past successes. The aged veteran soldier

> Shoulders his crutch, and shows
> How fields are won.

And why should not the veteran statesman speak of his exploits and victories? Senator ANTHONY was too modest to do this.

He outlived nearly all his early Senatorial colleagues. The names of Douglas and Yates of Illinois, Baker of California, Sumner of Massachusetts, Fessenden of Maine, Seward and King of New York, Chase, Wade, and Pugh of Ohio, Crittenden of Kentucky, Collamer of Vermont, Hale of New Hampshire, Carpenter and Howe of Wisconsin, Morton of Indiana, Chandler of Michigan, and many others equally distinguished have long ago been "carved on the marble that covers their dust." Rhode Island has buried but recently (September, 1881) another United States Senator—General Burnside. He was a soldier of renown as well as a statesman.

While both Senators ANTHONY and Burnside belonged to the State they so faithfully and ably represented, yet their fame and deeds belong now to the whole country, to freedom, to civilization, and to humanity.

Resolutions of the Military Order of the Loyal Legion, District of Columbia Commandery, adopted November 5, 1884.

HENRY BOWEN ANTHONY, a companion of the third class, died at his residence in Providence, on the 2d day of September, 1884.

Senator ANTHONY was born in Coventry, Rhode Island, April 1, 1815. His ancestors were among the oldest inhabitants of that town, their Saxon blood and Quaker principles indicating their origin and their character. Receiving a classical education, he was graduated from Brown University in 1833. His health failing, he relinquished his legal studies, and in 1838 he assumed the editorial charge of the Providence Journal and soon gave evidence of his common sense, his practical energy, and his varied learning, spiced with a refined humor that attracted the attention of the reading people of Rhode Island. No man in that State had a wider circle of devoted friends, and those who did not enjoy his personal acquaintance could say that—

> He, in a general honest thought,
> And common good to all, made one of them.
> His life was gentle, and the elements
> So mix'd in him that Nature might stand up
> And say to all the world, "This is a man!"

In 1849 Mr. ANTHONY was elected governor of the State of Rhode Island, and he was re-elected in 1850, but he declined being a candidate for a third term. His course as chief magistrate of his native State was marked by a strict attention to its material interests and devotion to the great principles of public liberty.

On retiring from the gubernatorial chair he again devoted his whole time to his editorial labors until 1859, when he was elected United States Senator. He took his seat in the Senate on the 5th of December, 1859, and continuously occupied it, having been successively re-elected in 1865, in 1871, in 1877, and in 1883. He was several times elected President *pro tempore*, and at the time of his death he was the *Pater Senatus.*

At the outbreak of the rebellion Mr. ANTHONY at once took a decided stand in defense of the Union. A typical conservative, and by birth a lover of peace, he faced the secession movement with unflinching firmness and advocated its unconditional defeat. The sagacity which prompted the decision which nerved and the resolution which supported him are stamped upon the legislative annals of the war for the restoration of the Union, and the soldiers and sailors of Rhode Island will ever cherish their recollections of his patriotic generosity.

Senator ANTHONY was not a frequent speaker, but when he addressed the Senate he was always listened to with attention. His eloquence was practical and sensible, with no attempt at worthless verbal embroidery, yet amidst its solid Senatorial sentences there was classic grace that engaged the ear, while his dignified presence, grace of manner, and pleasant voice aided in gratifying his audiences.

The commandery of the District of Columbia selected Senator ANTHONY as a companion of the third class, an honor which he highly appreciated. He was not, however, permitted to meet with the commandery many times. Death claimed him, and the summons had to be obeyed. His stalwart form, crowned with white locks, will no more be seen in the Senate Chamber; his kind heart is cold; his friendly hand is numb. It is pleasing to know that his mental faculties were bright, clear, and firm to the last, and he died in the mellow evening-shine of matured faculties, as he had lived, a philosopher, a gentleman, and a Christian.

Resolved, That this memorial be entered on the records of the commandery, and that a copy of the same be forwarded to the family of our late companion.

JOHN F. MILLER,
Brevet Major-General, U. S. V.,
HENRY J. SPOONER,
First Lieutenant, U. S. V.,
BEN: PERLEY POORE,
Major, M. V. M.,

} *Committee.*

Remarks by Mr. TUCKER, of Virginia.

Mr. SPEAKER: The death of Hon. HENRY B. ANTHONY, late Senator from the State of Rhode Island, who, by his long and distinguished public service and his private virtues, has entitled himself to this memorial consideration by the two Houses of Congress, recalls to our minds the relation of his mother Commonwealth to our Federal Union at the foundation of the Government and at the ordeal crisis of its history during the period in which he was her representative in the Senate of the United States.

"Rhode Island and the Providence Plantations" constituted one of the original thirteen States which, under the loose league of the Continental Congress and afterward under the Articles of Confederation, fought together for the independence of the American States. But when the convention of 1787 met in Philadelphia to frame a new Constitution for these United States Rhode Island was conspicuous for her absence from its counsels, and signalized her jealousy of any change in the terms of the Federal Union by declining to supersede the old Articles of Confederation by the Constitution of 1789. Eleven States only ratified that instrument, and without the concurrence of North Carolina and Rhode Island the new Government was launched upon its voyage under the new Constitution. For nearly a year North Carolina, and until June 16, 1790, Rhode Island, were not members of the new Union constructed upon the terms of the Constitution of 1789.

The accession of Rhode Island by the act of her convention dated May 29, 1790, was accompanied by declarations and demands of amendments, which evinced at once her jealousy for her rights as a State and her apprehension of danger from the powers delegated to the Federal Government.

She entered the Union as the equal of every other State in the Senate, but with only one vote in the House of Representatives. Shorn of her equipollent power in the House, and fearful of its effects upon the rights of the States and the liberties of her people, she declared in like terms with Virginia, and in the same terms with New York, "that the powers of Government may be reassumed by the people whensoever it shall become necessary to their happiness;" and she proposed amendments, which foreshadowed those subsequently adopted within a few years after the adoption of the Constitution, by which the reserved rights of the States were more explicitly secured, and the delegated powers of the United States were more clearly defined. In all of these views, Virginia, the then largest State, and Rhode Island, the then smallest State, were wholly in accord.

But in the next seventy years alienation of views and feelings were produced by diversity of interests, and from the existence of slavery in the South, to which the people of Rhode Island were strongly opposed. The tariff, the Missouri restriction, the relation of slavery to the Territories and to this District, engendered contentions which brought the Union to the crisis of 1860, about which time Mr. ANTHONY entered the Senate of the United States.

He was then about forty-five years of age and in the prime of his powers. A member of the Society of Friends, his political, personal, and religious sentiments made him a warm and earnest opponent of slavery. Originally a Whig and devoted adherent of Mr. Clay, he became a Republican when that party absorbed all opposition in the Northern States to the Democratic party. Of course he promoted the election of Mr. Lincoln in 1860, and supported with zeal and consistency all the measures for the war upon the Confederate States. At the close of the war he sustained the reconstruction measures and the entire policy of the party to which he belonged until his death in September, 1884.

It is difficult in any part of his political career for me to find a point of agreement between us. Without doubt there may have been questions on which we concurred, but they were few and on matters of minor importance.

But this variance of opinions, and even upon such questions as involved the two sections of the country in a civil war, cannot prevent me from offering my willing testimony to his talents, to the purity of his private character, to his incorruptible integrity as a Senator, to the sincerity of his convictions, to the patriotism of his intentions, and to the urbanity, dignity, and courtesy which distinguished his personal and official intercourse. I knew him not intimately, but well enough to appreciate his intellect, to admire his public and private virtues, and to pay willing tribute to his patriotic devotion to what he thought was for the best interests of his country.

And why should differences upon political questions stint our praise of men whose conscientious convictions were as pure and honest as our own? Why should the embers of civil strife kindle again a wall of fire between me and one who was from genuine patriotism an enemy during the four dreadful years of carnage and of devastation? Why shall not men of both sides ascend to the heights of a magnanimity of thought which will accredit to their one-time foe, but now their fellow-citizen and compatriot, as sincere convictions and as genuine purposes to maintain the right and uphold the truth as is claimed for themselves? Who professes infallibility in thought or action? What standard can we who are prone to err erect for pronouncing judgment on others? If others are honest in opinion and purpose, who of us shall dare to condemn them for opinions contrary to our own?

For myself I declare in the solemn presence of the dead that I can and do forget all the diversities and hostilities of the past, and accord to him as much of virtue in purpose and of conscientiousness in action as I claim for those to whom he was hostile. Let the dead past be thus buried in the graves of the dead of both sections, and let the living practice that noble charity which accords to every other what each claims for himself, and we will in honorable recognition of each other's virtues and forbearance for each other's faults move on with mutual respect and affection to the achievement of the best results for our common country in the grand future of the American States. It is thus, and only thus, that we can secure to the future of our country a true and genuine peace between the once hostile sections and make us one in heart and purpose, as we are one in constitutional Union. For myself, in all sincerity, I rejoice in this opportunity to testify these catholic sentiments and purposes, by laying upon the tomb of the late Senator from Rhode Island this chaplet which Virginia weaves through my humble hands as her tribute of honor to the character, virtues, and fame of the lamented dead!

Remarks by Mr. SPOONER, of Rhode Island.

Mr. SPEAKER: The "Father of the Senate" is dead. A long life of usefulness, largely devoted to the public service, has closed. A career unexampled by that of any son of his native State and almost unparalleled in the history of the Republic has terminated. All that was mortal of HENRY B. ANTHONY has been borne to its final resting place, reverently escorted by representatives of the National and State governments and by the mourning people of Rhode Island, and tenderly committed to the soil from whence he sprang.

His obsequies have been said; his virtues and attainments depicted, and his great services to his State and the nation fittingly portrayed. The General Assembly of the State of Rhode Island, the Board of Trade of the city of Providence, the Commandery of the Loyal Legion of this District, of which he was an honorary and an honored companion, the Senate of the United States, the public press, and the voice of the people have all recounted and recalled the incidents of his honorable life and pronounced their eulogies upon his private character and his distinguished public services.

The utterances of this hour, devoted to the memory of the deceased Senator, properly supplement the many similar tributes to his worth; and, though evolving little perhaps not already said, may at least, while giving appropriate recognition by this House of the public loss and the public sorrow, point again the lessons of a completed and well-spent life; and so, while appreciating the completeness of the tributes already paid, I cannot omit the opportunity offered to render this last testimonial of respect and regard for my late friend and colleague.

It was Senator ANTHONY's fortune to live in stirring, troublous times, and to be a prominent participant in events which have largely contributed to the making of our history. From early manhood to almost the allotted life of man he may be said to have been constantly concerned in the direction of public affairs; first as an influential editor and controller of public thought; then as governor of his State; and finally as United States Senator by five successive elections and during more than twenty-five years of continuous service, embracing the most eventful period of our national existence.

Liberally educated and graduating at Brown University in 1833, with great natural talents and no small degree of cultivation and adaptability for the work, Mr. ANTHONY five years later became sole editor of the Providence Journal, in which capacity he established that newspaper among the leaders of New England opinion, and attained his earlier reputation as a graceful, vigorous writer, and a keen and discriminating critic of men and of public affairs.

The period of his earlier editorial career was in those years which immediately preceded and included the so-called "Dorr rebellion," when wide and irreconcilable differences among the people of Rhode Island concerning their suffrage gave rise not only to bitter discussions and personal and party dissensions, but even to domestic strife and an appeal to arms, threatening the peace and the very existence of the State. In those days Mr. ANTHONY and his paper were the stern, uncompromising supporters of the so-called "Law-and-order" party of Rhode Island, urging the supremacy of existing law and of the government organized under it until the same should be changed by and through the instrumentality and processes which that law recognized, and earnestly demanding the suppression by armed force of any armed resistance to what they claimed to be the only lawful government of the State.

It was during that period that Mr. ANTHONY established his reputation as an editor and first illustrated the proportions of his ability and the grasp and insight of his intellect. Yet, bitterly as the conflict was waged between the "Dorrites" and the "Algerines," as the contending parties were called, and virulent as were many of the animosities and antagonisms aroused—families and former friends dividing in hostile array—and although no man in Rhode Island more persistently and vigorously opposed Thomas W. Dorr and his associates than did HENRY B. ANTHONY, his peculiar characteristics, both of manner and method, are illustrated by the fact that many of his most hostile opponents in those days of internal strife subsequently became his faithful political adherents and closest personal friends. Indeed, within a few days I have read a letter recently written by an old "Dorrite" and a strong political opponent of Mr. ANTHONY in the "days of '42," who there speaks of the deceased Senator as one among his "ideals of great men."

Largely by reason of the reputation earned and the political alliances with which he became associated during the years of and immediately succeeding the contest referred to, Mr.

ANTHONY was in 1849 nominated by the Whig party of Rhode Island and elected governor of the State; and in the following year re-elected to the same office, receiving upon this second election more than three-fourths of all the ballots polled—a marked evidence of his popularity with the people and of their satisfaction with his discharge of his duties as chief magistrate during his preceding term.

It is a peculiarity of Rhode Island politics, due I believe partly to the size of the State and partly to the characteristic independence of her people, that party lines are frequently broken for the expression of individual preferences, and votes often cast in direct antagonism to the nominal party affiliations of the voter; and Mr. ANTHONY, having perhaps to a greater extent than any other of his fellow-citizens a large following of personal friends, of varying shades of political opinion, captivated by his genial manners and won by his unquestioned integrity and the constancy of his friendship and his purpose, always found many staunch political supporters among those whose political alliances were usually widely at variance with his own; and, although originally a Whig and subsequently always a Republican, through the course of his long public life he enjoyed the continuous confidence and political support of many Rhode Island Democrats.

A Rhode Islander by birth and descended from old Rhode Island stock; by nature, descent, instinct, and education saturated with the ideas, principles, and convictions peculiar to the people of his State; with an affection akin to admiration for her traditions, her history, and her ancient institutions, Mr. ANTHONY was for more than a quarter of a century recognized as that one of all her citizens best qualified to represent her interests, as was evinced by his repeated elections to serve her

during all that period in the United States Senate. His Senatorial career, extending from 1859 to the time of his death in
September, 1884, spanned the lifetime of a generation. It saw
the rise and overthrow of the great rebellion, the abolition of
slavery, and the reconstruction of the Union, with constitutional liberty for black as well as white as a foundation-
stone; it witnessed the restoration of financial safety and
integrity and that wonderful expansion of American industries
which wise legislation had fostered; it beheld that marvelous
growth and prosperity which, within that period of time, had
nearly doubled the population of Rhode Island as well as the
population of the United States, and had nearly tripled the
value of their manufactured products; it saw the star of the
Republic, which had seemed about to set in clouds and dark-
ness, blazing again in the peaceful sky as a beacon-light to
progress and to freedom!

The long and faithful services of Senator ANTHONY in the
national councils form a conspicuous part of the recorded history of our country, and scarcely demand recital here. They
constitute a record of high patriotism, fidelity to duty, and
prudent statesmanship during those trying seasons of peril and
of strife when numerous new and important questions affecting
the safety and perpetuity of our institutions vexed the public
mind and demanded Congressional action; they embrace the
period following the war, when matters of scarcely less importance to the welfare, peace, and prosperity of our people—the
reconstruction of the Union, and questions of finance and
traffic and taxation—called for that wisdom in legislation
which he was so competent to exercise. Affable and courtly
in manner, earnest yet prudent and conservative, diligent in
the work committed to his charge, possessing rare gifts of

eloquence and persuasion as well as a logical mind united with unusual power of statement and analysis, Senator ANTHONY, though seldom indulging in formal speeches in the Senate and but infrequently engaged in debate upon the floor, was for many years a power in the affairs of Government and one of the most influential of Senators. As an industrious member and as chairman of important committees, and for four years as President *pro tempore* of the Senate, he has left the impress of his statesmanship and his patriotism upon much of the legislation enacted during his term of Senatorial service.

If Mr. ANTHONY had not been called to public life, but had continued to actively occupy his early editorial chair, I believe I may safely assert that he would have attained both reputation and fame as a great editor. That was a career for which he was peculiarly adapted and most admirably equipped by his ability, his inclinations, and his attainments.

Few men possessed a keener appreciation of men and motives or better understood the course and the cause of the progress of affairs, or could express their views more clearly, forcibly, and attractively. A master of good English, some of the earlier as well as the more recent products of his pen are among the best examples of correct and graceful diction which our literature affords. He could be witty without being offensive; humorous, and yet not gross; severe, but still kindly and discriminating; complimentary, yet not effusive; vigorous, or sympathetic, or critical, or sad, or gay; and through all he wrote there ever ran a genial, human vein, with a captivating style of thought and expression; and though his wit and satire were keen and incisive, yet, like the scimeter of Saladin, they seldom left a ragged wound to fester long after their blows had been delivered.

But I will delay the House no longer.

The "Father of the Senate" rests from his labors ; the voice of the master of eulogy is hushed ; and, with the memory of his glowing periods ringing in my ears, my simple tribute to his memory seems but discordant music.

His fame is a part of our common history, interwoven with the fame of Lincoln and Grant, and Seward and Sumner, and of those other patriots, now largely of the past generation, who labored, or fought, or died that the Union and free institutions might live.

Mr. Speaker, I move the adoption of the resolutions.

The resolutions were unanimously adopted ; and in accordance therewith (at five o'clock and ten minutes p. m.) the House adjourned.

○

www.ingramcontent.com/pod-product-compliance
Lightning Source LLC
Chambersburg PA
CBHW031158050726
47495CB00019B/2648